Gently Floating

Alan Hunter

ROBINSON

Constable & Robinson Ltd
55–56 Russell Square
London WC1B 4HP
www.constablerobinson.com

First published by Cassell & Co. Ltd., London, 1963

This edition published by Robinson,
an imprint of Constable & Robinson Ltd, 2012

A copy of the British Library Cataloguing in
Publication data is available from the British Library

ISBN: 978-1-78033-152-2 (paperback)
ISBN: 978-1-78033-153-9 (ebook)

Typeset by TW Typesetting, Plymouth, Devon

Printed and bound in the UK

1 3 5 7 9 10 8 6 4 2

For
PERCY HUNTER & SONS LTD
the yacht builders

The English Broads consist of but 150 miles of navigable waterways – not the 200 miles of the adman – and it is a forlorn hope that a favourite part of them can be used as the setting for a crime novel, and remain anonymous. So on this occasion I would like to remind you, with more emphasis than usual, that the characters and events in this book are fictitious; only the locale is sketched from life.

A.H.

Alan Hunter was born in ~~~~~~~~~~~ ~olk in 1922. He l~~~~~~~~~~~~~~~~~~~~~~~~~~~ work on his father's farm, spending his spare time sailing on the Norfolk Broads and writing nature notes for the *Eastern Evening News*. He also wrote poetry, some of which was published while he was in the RAF during the Second World War. By 1950, he was running his own book-shop in Norwich. In 1955, the first of what would become a series of forty-six George Gently novels was published. He died in 2005, aged eighty-two.

The Inspector George Gently series

CHAPTER ONE

THE BIG MAN left the office without noticing that he hadn't locked it and went straight across the darkened yard to where his launch lay at the quay. There he hesitated, stood frowning, breathing the mild night air. The air had the sweet timber smell of boatyards mingled with petrol and the odour of the river. He was Harry French. He owned the yard. The yard let ninety-six craft. This was the Tuesday of August Bank Holiday week and all ninety-six craft were out. He didn't know where they were, except two which were mooring at the quay. He had a son, John. He didn't know where John was. Though he thought he could guess about that.

He stooped to untie the launch's painter, changed his mind a second time: stood as before, breathing the air, looking out across the river. Nobody could have told Harry French how important were the impressions he was receiving. He was fifty-two. He had never thought very seriously about dying. He was highly successful with his business. He was not so successful with his family. His wife was dead. He had one son. His son didn't take to the business. It was around ten p.m. on August 4th. Like every other season. Almost.

For example, all the evening Reuben's fair had been pounding out music across the river, just as it had done every August Bank Holiday week since French had come to Haynor in nineteen twenty-four. Squeezed into the same pocket handkerchief between road, river and a mooring cut, the same ancient but virile Cakewalk rising above identical stalls. As a youth French had loved the Cakewalk and its challenging clatter of mechanical music; later, a parish councillor, he had tried to ban it; tonight, obscurely, it seemed a friend. Reuben, or Reuben's successor, had not been seduced by recorded music. The Cakewalk played tunes of the twenties and thirties. At the moment it was playing 'Donna Clara'.

Over the river, a little upstream, was this turgid violence of sound and light, beside the dark, heavy form of the hog-backed medieval bridge; and lining the quays, down both banks, the brooding whitenesses of moored craft, porthole lights reflecting from the water, a coal-blue sky empty above them. Traffic lights showed on the bridge, a double-decked bus rocked slowly over it. People moved along the bank, over the bridge, crowded under the fairground lights. 'Donna Clara', all the boats out. Like every other season, almost. Haynor or Harry French, either, it didn't matter; for Thou art That.

And nobody could have told him how important it was on this night of August 4th. Or why his identity came to him sharply as he stood on the quay, testing a decision.

The music changed to 'Harvest Moon'. At last he

2

jerked the painter from its ring. He stepped aboard the mahogany launch, on the coamings of which dew had formed. She rocked, butted the tyre-sections nailed to the quay to serve as fenders; moved a little downstream on the ebb while he found his seat and reached for the starter. The engine snatched, took hold. He fingered the light-switch, didn't press it. She remained a dark, low shadow, sliding softly from the quay. Pointing upstream, under the bridge, whose scarred stone arch bounced the murmur of her engine. By the shallow sheds of Spelton Bros., the empty tables on the Bridge Inn staithe. Towards the bungalows, huddled shack by shack on low plots between river and dyke. Towards the ghostly night of Haynor Sounds. Away from the big French house downriver.

But just above Spelton Bros. the launch drifted to her left, her engine idling at low throttle and barely stemming the weak ebb. French laid her close in, closer; found the ramshackle staithe for which he was searching. When she touched he cut the engine and stepped quickly ashore with the painter. He looked about him. The staithe fronted rough ground on which an old upturned boat lay decaying. Nothing moved there. Across the river lay a houseboat without lights. He hitched the painter to a post and moved silently across the rough ground. It was bounded by the cinder path which served the long string of bungalows. Down the path, towards the road, a light showed in one of the Speltons' sheds, up the path, no light. French went up the path. He counted the gates in the wooden fence which separated the backs of the bungalows from the path. At the seventh gate he stopped, stood by it motionless for some seconds. The seventh gate glimmered faintly. He knew it was painted a whitey-green. If it had been daylight he could have read the name Marshways painted on it. Reuben's Cakewalk was now playing 'Valencia' while French stood listening at the seventh gate.

He reached for the latch and pressed it softly. It was old, lifted sloppily. The gate itself had a creak which his gentle opening of it only prolonged. He went through. He stood in a cramped yard at the rear of the bungalow. It contained a square rainwater tank, an outside safe, a dustbin and a man's bicycle. On the right the bungalow butted hard on the fence of its neighbour. On the left was a narrow mooring cut in which lay a ten-foot dinghy. A light in the front of the bungalow fell on the sternsheets of the dinghy. It showed a seagull clamped on the transom. It was a dinghy belonging to French's yard. He moved to the back door of the bungalow, very close. A sing-song of voices came to him. One of the voices was a woman's, but that was all he could tell certainly. He looked for a way round to the front, but the only way was through the building. He listened again. Laughter. Suddenly he was near to vomiting.

Instead, French closed his eyes and took several long full breaths, then he felt over the surface of the door until his hand found the knocker. It was a little souvenir knocker in the shape of a pixie. He took hold of as much of it as he could and beat with it sharply six times. The sounds it gave out were trifling, but immediately the voices in the bungalow fell silent. He thought he heard

4

movement, a door open. He went on controlling his breathing. At last some steps, light knifing under the door, a hand fumbling with the bolt; then the door opening a foot to show the dark shape of a man. French crashed the door wide open. The man fell back from French's weight. French went in. He said: 'All right. I know he's here. Where've you hidden him?'

The man was a head shorter than French and half a dozen years younger. He had a solid body and wide shoulders and short legs and he was humpty. He had a tanned porous face with a big squashed nose and a broad, round chin. His eyes were grey under heavy lids which were creased with habitual puckering. He wore an open-neck khaki shirt and navy bib-and-brace overalls and a pair of plimsolls with holes in them. He had thinned black hair, but no baldness.

He backed a few steps down the narrow hallway which ran through the bungalow, then stopped. He filled the hallway. French was forced to stop too. The man was on the balls of his feet, long arms hanging loose. His eyes puckered to small dots. His wide mouth stretched in a loose grin.

He said softly: 'Now then, Harry, what sort of games are you playing at? You can't do this sort of thing, you know, not busting into a bloke's house.'

French said: 'You've got my son here. Don't try coming it with me, Sid.'

The man said: 'Suppose he is here? He's twenty-one, isn't he? Does what he likes?'

French came on. 'Just fetch him,' he said.

'Wait, now,' the man said, raising his hands. 'I didn't say he was here, Harry, did I? But he's got the right, you can't deny that.'

'Get out of my way,' French said.

'No,' the man said. 'Not in my own house. You may be the boss and all that caper, but you can't bust into a bloke's house.'

'I want my son.'

'Even so,' the man said.

'I'm going to have him,' French said.

'Not by busting in here you aren't,' the man said.

French looked at him. He felt the sickness again.

'Now just be reasonable a moment, Harry,' the man said. 'You can't push your boy around like this. He's got a mind of his own too – wouldn't be a French if he hadn't got that. He'll only hate you if you try to keep him down. And it won't do no good. He's twenty-one. And he's got this money coming along from his mother. What's the sense of trying to ride him?'

'Sid, you're sacked,' French said.

'It'll be a union job,' the man said.

'Union or not,' French said. 'You're sacked. Pick up your cards.'

The man shook his head. 'They'll be out. You won't get rid of me that way, Harry.'

'I'll not only sack you, I'll brand you,' French said. 'You'll never get another job on the yards.'

'It wouldn't work,' the man said.

'I'll have you out on the street,' French said. 'You're a pimp and a rogue and a corrupt influence. And you've seduced my son. I'll finish you, Sid.'

The man puckered his eyes. 'That'll do,' he said.

'Yes, I'll finish you,' French said. 'You're as rotten as they come, Sid. I knew it all along, you bloody lead-swinger you. But getting your hooks into John. You and that whore you call a wife.'

The man's eyes were like needle-points. 'Shut your trap and get out,' he said.

'I'm taking my son,' French said.

'You're getting out,' said the man.

He came at French, swinging. French grappled with him, glad of the combat. The man was strong, but he was much the lighter and French pitched him down on the hallway floor. The man squirmed up, swearing, murderous; rushed at French two-fisted. French poked a left into the man's chest, threw a right to the face with all his weight in it. The man went backwards. He spat blood. He looked about him for a weapon. There was an iron doorstop by the further door and he caught it up, came again. French rushed at him and caught his wrist before the man could strike a blow. He bent the man's arm back till he dropped the doorstop. The man screamed and went down after it.

'You vicious bastard,' French said. 'I'll break your bloody arm for you.'

'I'll do you in,' the man swore. 'I will. I will. I'll bloody kill you.'

'John!' French shouted. 'Come out. I know you're in here somewhere.'

He began throwing open the doors, but the second door he tried was locked. He hammered on it, shouting. The man was getting up off the floor. French drove his shoulder into the door and the door sagged. Then the man was on him.

'You bugger, you bugger!' the man was gasping.

He had the stop in his hand again. French seized his wrist but couldn't bend it back, took a numbing blow on the shoulder. He heaved at the man and shoved him away. The man stood swaying, panting, watching. The blow on French's shoulder had hurt. He didn't follow up to deal with the stop. The man threw it. It grazed French's arm and bounded up the hallway with violent bumps. French went forward, got a plimsoll in his stomach, staggered back a pace, winded, remained sucking in breath.

'You bloody great sod,' the man swore.

But he didn't attack French again. From three yards' distance they eyed each other, resting, breathing, calculating chances. Reuben's Cakewalk was blatting out 'Dark Eyes'. Some blood was dripping down the man's chin.

'Are you opening that door?' French gasped.

'Bloody great sod,' the man repeated.

'I don't go without him,' French said.

The man said nothing, made no move.

A door behind the man opened, but the man didn't turn his head. A blonde woman came out into the hallway. She stood still, looking at the two men.

'Aren't you bloody well ashamed?' she said.

'Shut your mouth, Rhoda,' the man snarled.

'I should shut my mouth,' she said, 'with you two behaving like wet kids. What's it about? You know John isn't here.'

8

'That's a damned lie!' French shouted.

'Clear out of here, Rhoda,' the man said.

The woman shrugged, made a swing motion with her hips.

'He hasn't been here,' she said to French. 'We haven't seen him this week.'

'He's in this room,' French shouted. 'Either you open it or I smash the door in.'

She felt in a pocket. 'Catch,' she said. She threw a small door-key to French. The man rounded on her, feinted a blow. She laughed in his face, didn't flinch away.

The room was a small, cheaply furnished bedroom with plasterboard-lined walls. It contained nowhere for a man to hide and there was nobody in it. One of its lattice windows was pegged open. French went across and looked through the window. It gave into a dark, narrow cul-de-sac which communicated with the front of the plot. Nothing stirred out there. The room had a bleak, unoccupied smell.

The blonde woman came into the room after French and stood near the door, watching him look through the window. She was about forty years old and wore a blue worsted dressing gown and she had an oval face with full features and she had a full figure and it was firm. She had steady blue eyes, a round-tipped nose and a crumpled mouth. Her blonde hair was naturally blonde. It had been fashioned by a hairdresser but now straggled untidily. She was smiling at French's back. When he turned she didn't smile.

She said: 'Satisfied?'

His brown eyes fastened on her. He came back from the window.

'He wasn't here,' the blonde woman said. 'Perhaps he's giving the girls a treat in town.'

'You lying whore,' French said to her.

'Thanks for nothing,' the woman said.

'You got him out of here,' French said. 'He must have taken a rowboat from the front.'

'We don't have a rowboat,' the woman said. 'Your bloody work-launch bust it up for us.'

'Liar, liar,' French said.

'Aren't you a sweet bastard,' the woman said.

'There's one of our dinghies in the dyke,' French said. 'Do you think I can't believe my eyes?'

The woman drew her head back to stare at him. 'And that's the bloody reason?' she said. 'You break in here and knock Sid about because of that dinghy in the dyke?'

'He came in that dinghy,' French said.

'Don't make me spit,' the woman said. 'Sid had that dinghy, his bike is buggered up. Mr Archer said he could borrow a dinghy.'

'To go quarter of a mile?'

'What's that got to do with it? They never walk when there's a boat.'

'You filthy liar,' French said.

'A gent,' the woman said. 'A gent.'

French closed his eyes. The woman watched him. The man was moving in another room. French's face showed pale, dragged. He was shifting his weight from side to side.

'It's got to stop,' he said, his eyes still closed. 'You won't get the money. I'll see to that. I'll get an injunction. You'll never see a penny. Did you think I'd let my son be robbed?'

'Who's talking of robbing him?' the woman said.

'His mother's money,' French said. 'I don't have to watch while you pinch it off him, while he's debauched by a bitch like you. Now I'm telling you. It's got to stop. Sid can pick up his money in the morning. And if ever I find John here again, I'll see you both out in the gutter.' He opened his eyes. 'You heard that?'

'You're up the pole,' the woman said. 'What do we care about your brat's money? You're a bloody joke, with your big talk.'

'I can fix you,' French said.

'Try scaring your son,' the woman said.

'And I can talk to the union,' French said. 'They won't wear the sort of game you're up to.'

'What game?' the woman said. 'Let's see your proof, if you've got any.'

French closed his eyes again, swallowed, tried to breathe regularly.

The woman said: 'Look, you're all mixed up. Nobody's trying to rob your precious son. And you've knocked yourself up, if you ask me, you'd better sit down and have a drop of something.'

'You've had your warning,' French said.

'Let's go and sit down,' the woman said. 'Christ knows, there's no harm in talking about it. Perhaps it'll make you feel better.'

She turned away from him, went down the hallway,

into the room on the left. The man was sitting in it. He was dabbing his mouth. His lips were cut and puffing up. She winked at the man.

'You frig off, Sid. I'll do better on my own.'

'If ever I get a chance at that bastard,' he said.

'Just frig off, I can handle him.'

The man muttered, got to his feet, went padding off down the hallway. As he passed French he spat on the floor. He slammed the door of the bungalow, and after it, the gate. The woman came out in the hallway, beckoned to French.

'Got a stinking temper, Sid has,' she said. 'But he'll get over it, it doesn't last. We can talk now he's gone.'

'You heard what I said,' French said.

'You're worked up too,' the woman said. 'I don't care what you've been saying. It's a lot of pills. Come and sit down. I'll tell you something about your son. You've worked yourself up about nothing.'

'You're a liar,' French said.

'I know I'm a liar,' she said. 'Come and sit down.'

French looked at her a long time. Then he went slowly along the hallway. The room on the left was furnished as a lounge and looked over a veranda which faced the river. The furniture was cheap and pre-war but there was a modern TV and a transistor radio. The room smelled of cigarette-smoke and of a cheap cosmetic. It was small and the furniture was huddled together. The woman went to a stained-wood cabinet and poured whisky into glasses from a Dewars' bottle. She added nothing to it. She handed one glass to French.

She said: 'Cheers,' and swallowed half her drink.

12

French didn't drink or say anything. She closed the door he had left open, sat on the settee, crossed her legs.

'So John's a nice boy,' she said.

'I don't want to hear about it,' French said.

'Don't be so bloody touchy,' she said. 'And sit down so I don't have to crick my neck. I want to talk to you.'

French looked behind him, found a fireside chair, sat.

'He's a nice boy,' she said. 'You're quite right, I made a man of him. What's wrong with doing that, anyway? Some fast little bitch might have got hold of him.'

'You're only twice his age,' French said.

'Don't give me that,' the woman said. 'That's what they want when they're that age – a woman who knows all about it. I've been bloody good for that boy – the way he is, shy. You ought to thank me instead of shouting at me. I've been an education to him.'

'And Sid holds the door?' French said.

'Sid,' the woman said. She made a gesture. 'Sid doesn't give a crap, he never did, about that. Maybe his accident did something to him.'

'It was his own fault,' French said.

'I know it was,' the woman said. 'For chrissake climb down a bit.'

'His own fault,' French said. 'He tried to walk a yacht up the slipway. Showing off to the apprentices. That's how he hurt his back. And I paid him compensation, though I wasn't damn well liable, and he's been swinging the lead ever since, and making trouble. That's Sid.'

'Am I saying it isn't?' the woman said. 'I should know what the bleeder's like.'

'And you're just the mate for him,' French said.

'Oh, bloody stick it,' the woman said.

She swallowed the second half of her drink and set the glass on the linoleum. Then she uncrossed her legs, hoisted them on the settee, lay back. Reuben's Cakewalk had closed down. Some distant pub turnouts were yelling. After that it was quiet. The river flowed without sound.

'Listen,' she said. 'You're making a hell of a lot of fuss about nothing. Some time your son was going after it, and he might have done a damn sight worse than me. And you don't like Sid. So bloody what? He doesn't slay me either. But you've got him wrong about pinching the kid's money, he isn't a rogue. It's a bit of business.'

'Business,' French said.

'What's the use of being so bloody sour?' she said. 'The kid gets on with Sid if you don't, and it's all fair and above board.'

French looked at her.

'All right,' she said, 'you want to know what it is? You don't trust Sid and me, do you, but I'll show you we can trust you. It's Jimpson's dance hall, that's what, over the other side of the bridge.'

'What about the dance hall?'

'That's the idea,' she said. 'Running the dance hall again.'

'That wreck?'

'It wants doing up,' she said. 'But it'll pay, don't you worry.'

After a pause, French said: 'I'll buy it. I'll tear it down and make a car park.'

'Oh, no you don't,' the woman said. 'Sid's got an option. Molly Jimpson's his cousin.'

'I'll buy the option,' French said. 'Is that what you're after? How much?'

'We're not bloody selling,' the woman said. 'So you can stick that idea. This is business, like I said. And your son's coming in on it. Why the hell shouldn't he branch out if he wants to? He doesn't give a frig for the boats.'

French closed his eyes, said: 'I'll find a way to fix that. Option or not, I'll fix it. I'll get my son clear of you.'

'Be your age,' the woman said. 'Didn't I trust you, telling you about it?'

'Your mistake,' French said. 'You whore. I'm glad I let you talk.'

'Now look here,' the woman said. She sat up. 'I've been straight with you, Harry. I told you that in bloody confidence. Sid would knock me about if he knew. So why not play ball?'

French came to his feet.

'You might as well as not,' the woman said. 'The kid'll hate you if you bugger it up, and he'll perhaps do worse, just to spite you. Can't you be a bit bloody human? Let other people live too? I should think a woman would do *you* good, living alone in that damn great house.'

'You?' French said.

'What's wrong with me?'

French put down his glass on the table.

'I'd sooner take a bath in a cesspit,' he said.

'You'd smell about the same if you did,' the woman said.

They looked at each other.

'Sid's sacked,' French said. 'He needn't come in. I

15

don't want to see him. I'll send his money and cards round.'

'Get stuffed,' the woman said. 'I hope a bus runs over you.'

He turned, went straight through the door, down the hallway, out of the bungalow. When the gate slammed behind him he took a few steps down the cinder path, came to a stand. He was trembling. A faint night breeze pressed over the marshes from the direction of the Sounds, very soft, not enough to stir the leaves of a bush willow. Reuben's blaze had been dipped. The traffic lights were switched off. Only Spelton Bros.' shed showed a dim panel of light. French took several steady breaths, feeling the pulses beat in his temples. The trembling didn't decrease. His bruised arm and stomach ached. The little breeze carried a fragrance of reeds, water, marsh-litter, forcing an image of the Sounds through the obsession in his mind. He let it lay there as he breathed. Then the pulsing, trembling, receded. He walked on down the path and across the rough ground to the staithe. The launch lay downstream, streamed on the ebb. He loosed the painter, reached for the coaming. The Sounds were still in his mind. When everything vanished.

Everything: the Sounds, the obsession underlying them, French's body, the launch, the river, the night; the ninety-six craft, all let, the quays, the bridge, Reuben's Cakewalk, the yard, the memory of his wife, his house, his son, the big sky. Out, out, out, out. Not even distant memories left. Not the wide country nor the ocean nor the world's rim nor the stars. Thou art

That was so no longer, the stubborn deception resolved: the one appearing two now the one appearing one. And the appearance of the two vanished, vanished, vanished, vanished.

The launch went down on the ebb and found its way through the bridge, touched gently at dark quays, at the boats moored to them. It moved slantways and sideways, but never directly ahead; strayed small and soundless among the tall-sided cruisers. By the slack, which was near dawn, it was down below the bungalows, the downstream bungalows which stretched for a mile. A white mist was on the river. The launch was wet, dark, still. It had its stem to the reeds as though come to a mooring. Then the sun rose, at first redly, spilling into the wide marshes, thinning the swirling smoke vapour, warming the tones of the reeds; touched the launch's deep mahogany and its smart red plastic-covered cushions and its terylene painter hanging down in the water. The reed birds began to sing. A heron heaved up with broad slow wings. The heron wheeled to inspect the launch, carried its legs across the river. The mist collapsed, lower, lower, rolled along the surface, flattened, dissolved; the launch lay sharp and hard on the film of pale water. At half past five an angler rowed by. He stared at the launch, sat letting his blades drip. Then he pulled over, came alongside, saw the launch was empty, tied on to it.

Thus: the launch was returned to the yard and the angler left a note on it and resumed his angling. Later the note was seen by a yard-hand called Nunn who took it to the office and gave it to the manager. The manager's name was William Archer. He gave the French house a ring. He talked to the son, John French, who told him that French had apparently not returned to the house. Then the manager frowned, sat thinking, got up, made some inquiries around the yard, discovered that French had been at the office the previous evening, that the office had been found unlocked in the morning. He took the yard foreman with him and searched the yard. It was staring hot midday by then. The two men sweated as they climbed ladders, peered into lofts smelling of tar, timber, canvas. They found a suit of sails which had been missing since Whitsun, but they found no body turning on a rope. The manager returned to the office to telephone, found John French waiting there. John French was nervous.

Thus: the Haynor police constable was called from his lunch, and the River Police were informed and sent a patrol boat to Haynor. The two authorities conferred. From the known facts they evolved a theory. It was that Harry French fell in and was drowned when embarking in his launch to drive home from the yard. The River Police approximated the area of search, impressed two rowboats, sank their grapnels. People watched from the bank, from the bridge. Yard-hands came to the quay, watching. Mr Archer was kept busy in the office. John French was not in the office, nor watching. The dragging went on from three till six p.m. in the reach from the bridge to the first bend downstream. At six p.m. a message came from Speltons. The body had been found submerged in their downstream slipway. Down-stream for Speltons, upstream from the bridge: but the movements of a body under water have not been reduced to an exact science.

Thus: the police took charge of the body and laid it in Speltons' rigger's shop. They telephoned, stood by. A police Wolseley arrived from Starmouth. One of the men who got out of it carried a black leather bag. This was at ten minutes to seven. At seven p.m. there was more telephoning, and two of the men out of the car went across to French's office. They saw the manager, asked for John French, asked questions, did further telephoning. Until very late they were in the office, so that tea and sandwiches were sent over from the restaurant. Afterwards two of them went to the French house. Meanwhile, the launch lay where the angler had tied it.

Thus: on Thursday August 6th a conference was held at Police Headquarters, Starmouth, at which it was decided to request the assistance of an expert from the Central Office.

Thus: the Central Office instructed Superintendent George Herbert Gently to proceed to Starmouth and to provide such assistance.

The weather continued fine, with heavy dews at night.

CHAPTER TWO

SUPERINTENDENT GENTLY LEFT London on the A12 and drove through Ipswich and along the coast to Starmouth. He drove alone. He stopped at a café in Saxmundham for an iced drink. He arrived at Starmouth at four-thirty p.m. and drove directly to the County Police Headquarters in Trafalgar Road. He parked in a slot in front of Headquarters, put on his jacket, went in. The desk sent an usher with him to the first floor, to the office of Superintendent Glaskell. He met Glaskell. Glaskell sent for his C.I.D. Inspector Parfitt. Neither of these men were wearing jackets. Gently took off his jacket again. They sat. Glaskell said:

'Parfitt has been on the case since yesterday. He's pretty sure who the chummie is, but we haven't found a way to make it stick. The trouble is getting hard facts. On circumstantial evidence we might nail him. No weapon, nothing like that. We need a breakthrough badly.'

'Yes,' Gently said. He looked at Glaskell. Glaskell was a heavy-featured, balding man. He had a thickly boyish face and green-grey eyes that protruded slightly. Parfitt was big-boned, level-shouldered, had a large face with a pointed jaw. He had light-blue eyes. They stared intently. Neither man had smiled when shaking hands.

Glaskell said: 'They'd have given you the facts, would they? An outline, something like that?'

'Merely an outline,' Gently said. 'I've seen the press accounts, of course.'

'Yes, those,' Glaskell said. 'French was a V.I.P. of sorts. His yard is one of the biggest in the Broads. Did a lot of Admiralty work during the war. Plenty of money. Wife died last year. Now his son collects everything.' He cleared his throat. 'That's it,' he said. 'They didn't get on, and now the son collects.'

'I see,' Gently said. 'What's his alibi?'

Glaskell grunted, Parfitt moved his shoulders.

'About as weak as it can be,' Glaskell said. 'Only, let's face it, we can't break him. Parfitt had an all-night session with him. Parfitt's good at interrogation. The chummie was lying like an idiot, but he stuck to the tale. And no witnesses.'

'Still, what's the alibi?' Gently said.

Parfitt said: 'He was out sailing.'

Gently thought, said: 'Sailing in the dark?'

'That's right,' Parfitt said. 'It's what he says. He took out a half-decker after tea, went up to Hickstead and back. He'd be breaking the by-laws, sailing without lights, but that doesn't concern us. He'd have got back to Haynor at about eleven-thirty p.m., then he walked back to the house and got there at midnight. He knocked on the door of the housekeeper's bedroom, asked her where he could find some cold sausage. But he knew darned well where to find the cold sausage. He was just making sure she knew when he came in.'

'Yes,' Gently said, 'but how does that cover him? The E.T.D. was between nine p.m. and midnight.'

'It covers him this way,' Parfitt said. 'We've got a witness to when Harry French left his office. One of the French boats was moored there and the hirer was using the phone-box. He'd met French when he took over the boat and he saw him come out of the office at around ten p.m. French had switched off the office light and he went straight across the yard to the quay. The hirer was using the phone-box till ten-thirty p.m., then he went back to his yacht. French's launch had been moored near the yacht when the hirer went to phone but it was gone when he returned. So French must have been killed at about ten p.m., when the son says he was still upriver.'

Gently nodded. He said: 'You're accepting the theory that French was killed as he embarked.'

'I can't see anything else for it,' Parfitt said, 'unless it was arranged to look like an accident. But it could hardly have been that, with that sort of head injury. Nobody was going to think that French did it when he fell in.'

'How about the bruising?' Gently said.

'I don't know,' Parfitt said. 'If there'd been a fight it would have attracted attention. I can't see there having been a fight. But someone could have bashed him and he slipped in, and nobody noticed the splash. Nobody did notice a splash. Unless they'd gone before we talked to them.'

22

'Was there any sign of a struggle in the launch?' Gently asked.

'None,' Parfitt said. 'Nor on the quay.'

'In the office?' Gently said.

'Nor there either,' Parfitt said. 'Dr Thomas had a look at the son, and there was no evidence that he'd been fighting. He couldn't have stood up to French anyway. We reckon the bruising doesn't come into it. Perhaps French took a knock off something, it's easy enough in a boat-yard. Anyway, he was bashed from behind. We reckon chummie crept up on him.'

'Can I see the photographs?' Gently said.

Parfitt opened a box-file he'd brought with him. He handed Gently a sheaf of glossy full-plate prints. They showed Harry French and his injuries. Harry French's skull had a depressed fracture about an inch above the nape of the neck. It was a circular depression, almost regular, not more than two inches in diameter at its widest.

'Blunt instrument,' Glaskell said, looking at the prints over Gently's shoulder.

'What sort of blunt instrument?' Gently asked.

'Something heavy with a knob on it,' Glaskell said. 'Probably a hammer, that's the most likely. There's plenty of hammers about a boat-yard, and chummie would know where to lay hands on one. Too many hammers, that's the trouble. He only had to wipe it and put it back.'

'Is there a hammer missing at the yard?' Gently asked.

'Not that we've heard of,' Parfitt said. 'We took away a hammer from the French house, but it was a snob's hammer, didn't fit. We looked at some at the yard. Perhaps chummie slung it in the river.'

'What do you make of the position of the injury?' Gently said.

Parfitt looked at him, said nothing.

'Wouldn't you expect it higher up the skull,' Gently said, 'a blow with a hammer, descending.'

'I don't know,' Parfitt said, 'if he was stooping to get in the launch. Then the back of his head would be uppermost, he'd get the injury there.'

'But if he wasn't stooping,' Gently said.

Parfitt shrugged, said: 'That's the way we see it.'

'How tall is the son?' Gently asked.

'About five ten,' Parfitt said.

'Let's send for a hammer,' Gently said. 'I'd like to get this point clear.'

Parfitt went out to fetch a hammer. Gently looked at the photographs again. Glaskell watched Gently looking at the photographs. He didn't say anything while Parfitt was out. Parfitt came back with an old, rusty hammer, and Gently rose, laid down the photographs. He said to Parfitt:

'I'm six feet tall, you'd be about five eleven. How tall was French?'

'Six one,' Parfitt said.

'I'll need to raise myself a couple of inches,' Gently said. He took a telephone directory from Glaskell's desk, laid it on the floor, stood on it.

'Now come behind and hit me,' he said to Parfitt. 'Don't hit me hard. It's too hot.'

Parfitt grinned very slightly. He went behind Gently,

swung the hammer. He let it come to rest delicately on Gently's skull. It lay on a spot at the top of the skull.

'Now,' Gently said, 'suppose you're a woman. It doesn't take a superman to kill with a hammer. Bend your knees till you're six inches lower, then you'll be relatively five six. Then try it again.'

Parfitt tried it again. The hammer came to rest just above Gently's nape. Gently stood off the directory, put it back on the desk. Glaskell was frowning at the hammer. He moved the directory slightly.

'So you think we're wrong about the son,' he said to Gently. 'But there's nobody else in the picture, and he's lying. You talk to him.'

'I don't think you're wrong,' Gently said. He smiled. 'I'm only fact-finding,' he said. 'It probably happened the way you think, but it's useful to know about the alternatives. Let's talk around it a bit. Give me some background stuff.'

'Parfitt can give it to you,' Glaskell said. 'He comes from that direction anyway.'

Parfitt set the hammer on the floor so that it balanced, handle up, then he sat. He glanced at Gently, let his glance slant sideways.

'I don't come from Haynor,' he said. 'I don't know everything that goes on there. But I was brought up in a Broads village and they're all about the same. This boat-letting trade is pretty recent, most of it's grown up within living memory. So you get men who went to school together in a boss and employee relationship. So there's jealousy and friction. The boss has to put up with a lot of familiarity. Also there's a shortage of skilled boatbuilders, and the men can afford to be independent. Maybe it keeps the industry healthy, I wouldn't know about that. It seems to work pretty well. While the boss keeps in line.'

'It's an expanding industry,' Glaskell said. 'That's why the skilled men are having it good. When the National Parks Commission scuttled from the Broads it was a signal for exploitation. Go to Blackpool. It's quieter. Better policed. More dustbins.'

'And probably fewer drownings,' Parfitt said. 'A drowning was rare when I was a kid.'

Gently nodded. 'I see,' he said. 'And what sort of a boss was French?'

Parfitt moved his shoulders. 'A bit uppity,' he said. 'That's what Reeve says. He's the constable at Haynor.'

'How?' Gently said.

'Well,' Parfitt said. He slid a look at Gently, and away. 'French threw his weight about,' he said. 'He didn't like his men being familiar. He was a foreigner, of course. But he'd lived in Haynor since he was a kid. His old man moved there from Beccles way and worked a while for Speltons. Then he started the yard over the road. Speltons were the big people at that time. Old man French was a fine designer and he went ahead between the wars. Harry French was more of a businessman, and he took over in thirty-eight. Harry French got the Admiralty contracts, expanded right, left and centre. Now it's Speltons who are the small yard. Harry French was a big man.'

'A big man,' Gently said.

'Yes,' Parfitt said. 'A big man. Don't get me wrong,

he was pretty all right, but he was a big man. That's how he was.'

Gently said: 'Who did he marry?'

'One of the Spenlows,' Parfitt said.

'They're county people,' Glaskell said. 'They do a lot of sailing. She had money.'

'So you'd say he married above him,' Gently said. 'That wouldn't make him popular either.'

'Don't suppose it did,' Glaskell said. 'They're a bloody independent lot round here.'

'The son takes after his mother,' Parfitt said.

'Yes,' Gently said, 'tell me about the son.'

'He's a bit of a, you know,' Parfitt said. 'He's a bit wet. And he lies like a bastard.'

'Is he in the business?' Gently said.

'Not from what I could make out,' Parfitt said. 'He's at Cambridge for another year, for whatever good it's going to do him. That's what half the rows were about, him being too good to go into the business. He was to have picked up some money his mother left him. Now he gets it all, of course.'

'So he wasn't at the yard much?' Gently said.

'Oh yes he was,' Parfitt said. 'Reeve says his old man kept a short rein on him, had him holding tools for the yard men. Don't worry, there's plenty of motive there. If we could get something to back it.'

'What else do you know about him?' Gently said.

'Runs after the women, doesn't he?' Glaskell said.

Parfitt shifted. 'Not exactly,' he said. 'He doesn't have enough guts to run after them. But he's been hanging round the village whore, whether he's got anywhere or

27

not. She's the wife of one of the yard-hands. Lidney. A red-hot momma, I've seen her. Nobody knows whether his father knew about it, but there'd have been hell to pay if he did.'

'What about French,' Gently said. 'Any gossip there?'

Parfitt's head shook. 'None,' he said. 'French was a one-woman man. I've talked to his housekeeper, Playford, you'll see her statement here. French was wrapped up in his wife. She was a fine-looking woman. She led him a dance, by all accounts, but he thought none the less of her for that. She died of anaemia last year. Her death hit French hard. He got broody, evil-tempered, tougher on his son. The son was a bit of a lost sheep, his mother didn't care for him either, but she found money for him to throw about. He's been having it thin since she died. He didn't go to her funeral, by the way, and there was a row about that.'

'What a hell of a family,' Glaskell said. 'You'll get me feeling sorry for chummie in a minute.'

'You'd be wasting it, sir,' Parfitt said. 'There's nothing sweet about chummie.'

'Has chummie any record of violence?' Gently asked.

No,' Parfitt said, 'not that we know of. But he gives you the impression he could slip you a quick one if you turned your back on him. I try to be fair, sir, where I can. But this one I just do not like. I know he did it. I'm bloody certain. And it makes me mad I can't nail him.'

'Yes,' Gently said. He stared out of the window a few moments. 'Getting back to the launch and the body,' he said. 'What can you tell me about that?'

'Well,' Parfitt said. 'The launch,' he said. 'That was

picked up below the bungalows. The ebb was running till three-thirty a.m. and there wasn't any wind. That'd probably be right, so the River Police tell us. If it went adrift from French's quay at about ten p.m., it would finish up a mile or so downstream. It might have backed a little on the first of the flood. It wasn't picked up till near five a.m.'

'And the body?' Gently said.

Parfitt's shoulders moved. 'That's not so easy. It was on the bottom, you can only guess what happens down there. But they reckon it didn't shift much until the boats began to move, then it was sucked up through the bridge by the afternoon flood. It's a narrow bridge, there's a strong current through it and it's scoured and deep under the arch. Then the water fans out after it gets through and pushes flotsam towards the bank. So the body got trapped in the slipway. That's how the River Police see it.'

'I see,' Gently said, looking out of the window again. Then he said: 'So the launch might have drifted a greater or a lesser distance.'

'Well, yes,' Parfitt said. 'You can't be precise with that sort of thing.'

'It would touch here and there, might get stuck for a while.'

'Yes,' Parfitt said. 'It wouldn't go straight down.'

'And the body,' Gently said. 'You were dragging for it below the bridge, weren't you?'

'The River Police did it,' Parfitt said. 'They know pretty well where to drop the hooks.'

'But this theory of theirs of how it was sucked

29

through the bridge, that was something that came afterwards?'

'Well, of course,' Parfitt said. 'They wanted to figure out how it got there.'

'From below the bridge.'

'Yes,' Parfitt said. He looked at Gently. Gently looked out of the window.

Glaskell said to Parfitt: 'I suppose it's just possible that French wasn't knocked off at the quay, drove somewhere else in the launch, ran into trouble there?'

'I don't see how,' Parfitt said. 'Nobody saw the launch going anywhere. It's got nav lights and a big searchlight and there were lots of people around to see it. There were boats all down the quays and Reuben's fair at the bridge. We talked to a score of people who were there. Nobody saw the launch take off.'

'Perhaps he didn't use his lights,' Glaskell said.

'He always used them,' Parfitt said. 'He used the launch as a sort of car to drive between his home and the yard. It's a very swish launch. Everyone knew it. He used to annoy people with using the searchlight. I talked to the manager, Archer, about it. French never drove it at night without the lights.'

'Say just this once,' Glaskell said.

'I think it very unlikely, sir,' Parfitt said. 'But even if he did, someone must have seen him. And they'd have heard the engine if they didn't see him.'

'You mentioned somebody's fair,' Gently said.

'Yes, Reuben's fair,' Parfitt said.

'What sort of a fair is it?' Gently said.

'Oh, just a small one,' Parfitt said.

'Any music?' Gently said.

'Yes, plenty of that,' Parfitt said.

'Pretty loud, is it?' Gently said.

Parfitt nodded, didn't say anything.

'I'd call it bloody loud,' Glaskell said, 'if it's the one I know. And it is. What's upstream of Haynor Bridge, Parfitt?'

Parfitt hesitated before saying: 'There's a shed of French's. Speltons' yard. The Bridge Inn opposite. The bungalows.'

'A shed of French's?' Glaskell said.

'Where they keep their half-deckers,' Parfitt said.

'Where they keep their half-deckers,' Glaskell said. 'That's a bloody alternative for you, isn't it? Suppose he'd gone there to meet his son coming back from this moonlight sail of his, and there was a row, and the son bonked him. That'd cover the facts, wouldn't it?'

'Yes,' Parfitt said.

'With the son admitting being out in a half-decker,' Glaskell said. 'You don't have to break his story. You have to build it up, Parfitt.'

Parfitt didn't say anything.

'Is that the idea?' Glaskell said to Gently.

Gently grinned at one and the other of them. 'I wouldn't know that,' he said. 'Your inspector's the man who's been on the job. He'll know the feel of things best. He's got a very good grasp on the situation plus the local knowledge that counts.'

Glaskell stared at Gently, chuckled. 'All right,' he said. 'Stop buttering him up. He's a good man. I'd back him anywhere. Just don't give him a swelled head.'

'I'm not saying I'm right, sir,' Parfitt said.

'Shut up, Parfitt,' Glaskell said.

'Yes, sir. Certainly, sir,' Parfitt said.

'You son of a bitch,' Glaskell said.

They laughed.

Gently said: 'That's about all till I've had a look round. I'll take your statements to read over and drive out after tea.'

'Come home with me,' Glaskell said. 'I've got orders from Marion to invite you. The town stinks. We're up the coast. Give you a look at the sea. What are you doing, Parfitt?'

'I'll have a meal here,' Parfitt said.

'Oh, to hell with that,' Glaskell said. He put his hand on the phone.

Thus: Superintendent Gently went to tea with Superintendent Glaskell and Inspector Parfitt, and tea was provided by Marion, Mrs Glaskell, on a paved terrace, under a sun-awning. So that when Superintendent Gently had washed and begun to feel comfortable, he was invited to sit at a table which looked across a lawn and over some sand dunes to the North Sea. The sand dunes were fawny yellow and stippled with marram grass, which was chalky green, and the North Sea was a high wall of emerald, purple, straw and heliotrope. On the edge of this wall, very bluish, tiny ships moved north and south, and from it blew a soft breeze which smelled of seaweed and the marrams. They ate lobster salad. The lobsters had been caught and boiled locally that morning. When they had eaten Superintendent Gently read the statements which Parfitt had taken. They were very dry reading, but Superintendent Gently was an expert reader. As he read he asked Parfitt questions about the people who had made the statements. Marion, Mrs Glaskell, didn't make the mistake of serving coffee. At six-thirty p.m. Superintendent Gently and Inspector Parfitt left the terrace. When Superintendent Glaskell returned from seeing them off he said something to his wife, who looked pleased.

They took the Moorford road from Hamby, driving almost straight inland. It was a narrow country road between stunted hedges of hawthorn. Beyond the hedges lay fields of stubble and fields of wheat and fields of barley, and in two of the fields lurched orange-painted combines, pushing out rectangular bales of straw. Amongst the wheat and the barley poppies grew and the air smelled of straw and poppies and dust. The sun was in front of them, low but brilliant. Air lay melted in dips of the road.

Parfitt said: 'Will you see anyone tonight?'

'No,' Gently said. 'Tomorrow.'

'Don't pay too much attention to what I say,' Parfitt said. 'It's new to me, all this.'

Gently said nothing.

'When you come to think of it,' Parfitt said, 'I've only been on the case twenty-four hours. Just rushed in and got a lot of impressions. I reckon I could have been too hasty.'

'We all feel like that,' Gently said.

'You fetched me up short,' Parfitt said. 'I can see now

I wasn't certain at all, just rushing in there and picking out a chummie.'

Gently kept driving.

'I think I panicked,' Parfitt said.

Gently kept driving. Parfitt was silent.

They passed through Moorford, struck the Stallbridge Road. The marshes lay flat ahead across the fields. The marshes were pale green and pale fawn and pale brown and very level and very wide and found their own horizon. Peaked rectangles of sails stood small across the marshes. The sails were white sails but cowslip-coloured in the evening sun. The sails moved very little. Sometimes a patch of willow or alder hid one. Two windpump towers without sails rose, bluish-ochre, far south. Coming to the marshes, the road dipped and ran flat between dykes and pollard willows. It approached a group of buildings of painted timber which stood squarely, flat-topped. From each side of this group stretched close-packed lines of low hutments with painted roofs and in the centre the road lifted over a narrow stone bridge. To the left of the bridge striped awnings clustered. Above them a wooden-valanced canopy sparkled with light bulbs. Also to the left rose a handful of masts at the trucks of which small triangular flags hung drooped.

'This is it,' Parfitt said. 'That's Reuben's, that is.'

A pulse of rhythm, overlaid with sprightly brass, grew towards them.

'Is the fair a regular event?' Gently said.

'Ever since I can remember,' Parfitt said. 'Every August Bank Holiday week it's here. It tours the other villages too.'

They came to the bridge, were halted by lights. The music bumped and clashed at their elbow. Through the stalls could be seen two elevated gangways which oscillated alternately in time with the music. At each side of the bridge the river appeared, narrow, across it gable-ended boat-sheds. Motor-cruisers and yachts were close-moored along the quays. A motor-cruiser and a launch were passing upstream, below the bridge.

The lights changed. Gently drove over.

'There,' Parfitt said, nodding to the right.

Gently drove on to a gravelled park on which a number of other cars were standing. Behind it a large single-storeyed timber building presented double glass doors and a range of windows. Over the doors were gilded wooden letters: HAYNOR COUNTRY CLUB (*Residential*). Gently fetched an attaché case from the boot. They went into the club. Gently checked in. Parfitt smoked in the lounge. Gently rejoined him there.

'Where to?' Parfitt said.

'I'd like to stand on the bridge,' Gently said.

'We'll probably get knocked down,' Parfitt said. 'The bridge doesn't cater for being stood on.'

They went on to the bridge, stood facing downstream, pressing close to the grey parapet. The reach downstream was a short one and was fenced at the bend by shanty bungalows. On the left was a stretch of bare rond with a capped timber quay-heading, on the right the quays, sheds and cuttings of Harry French's yard. On the tallest flat-topped building, in blue letters, stood: HARRY FRENCH & SON, YACHTS.

'So,' Gently said.

'Down there,' Parfitt said, 'where the cut goes into the yacht basin. Where *Caress 2* is moored. He was tied up on that corner.'

'Where's the office?' Gently said.

'In the tall building with the name on it,' Parfitt said. 'You come across by the toilets and a couple of store-sheds and over two bridges over slipways and along the quay.'

'There are no buildings on the quay,' Gently said.

'No,' Parfitt said. 'It'd be dark.'

'There'd be a certain amount of light from the fair,' Gently said. 'You'd see anybody on the quay with you.'

'It dazzles a bit,' Parfitt said. 'French was going towards it. It was in his eyes. I think it's possible for chummie to have nipped up behind him. If he was wearing yacht shoes, too.'

'Hmn,' Gently said. 'Who lives in that bungalow?'

'It's let,' Parfitt said. 'They're mostly let. I talked to the people, they didn't hear anything. They were watching television. They come from Bradford.'

Gently looked along the quays, down into the water. The evening flood rippled softly under the arch. The water was yellowish-brown when separated from its reflections, carried small flotsam below its surface. Two cars went by a few inches behind them. Gently said:

'You wouldn't linger here after dark. Not to notice a launch without lights going below. With all this noise and light beside you.'

'But people going along the bank,' Parfitt said. 'They'd have the light behind them, they might have noticed.'

'They might have noticed him being killed too,' Gently said. 'Only they didn't, or there'd surely have been a disturbance. Look, even with this row going you'd hear the splash of a body going in, perhaps even up here. When someone falls in there's a thumping splash, people stick their heads out to see if help's needed. And there was this yacht moored next door to the launch, but the statements say they didn't hear a splash. So there wasn't a splash. He must have fallen in without one. And he was a very large man to do that.'

'Chummie might have eased him in,' Parfitt said.

'Try it some day,' Gently said. 'Let's have a look over the other side.'

They crossed to the other parapet. The upstream reach was longer than the downstream. Adjacent to the bridge, on the left, was a wet boathouse, in which were moored five half-deckers with their masts lowered on crutches. Next came a run of shallow boat-sheds with five gables facing the river, beneath each gable sliding doors and slipways slanted into the water. Red lettering across the gables said: SPELTON BROS. YACHTS – HALF-DECKERS – ROWBOATS. Beyond these, rough rond, some small sheds, then the bungalows to infinity. On the right bank stood the Bridge Inn. It was an Edwardian brick-and-timber building. It had a quay-headed lawn to which hire launches were moored and on which stood metal tables and chairs where yachters sat with glasses and tankards before them. Next, small boat-sheds, cuttings. Next, quay-headed rond moored to capacity. Next, some store-sheds, a bit of rond with a houseboat; and the bungalows to infinity. The infinity of the bungalows curved to the right where it could be seen again, receding into the marshes.

'French's,' Parfitt said, pointing to the wet boathouse.

'Yes,' Gently said. 'Straight across from the inn.'

'I couldn't get anything there,' Parfitt said. 'Nobody was on the lawn after half past nine. The staff rooms are at the back. They've got some fishermen upstairs. One of them was about till after eleven, but he didn't notice anything going on over here.'

'Perhaps there was nothing to notice,' Gently said.

Parfitt moved his shoulders. 'That's my theory,' he said. 'I don't believe young French's alibi. And I don't believe French was knocked off here. It might look good in the Super's office, but not when you run a rule over the layout.'

'Then what are we left with?' Gently said. 'I don't think he was knocked off at the quay. I think he came upstream in the launch. Without lights. Where was he going?'

Parfitt moved his shoulders again. 'Speltons. It's the only obvious answer. And the body turned up in their slipway. It couldn't have happened far away.'

'Unless,' Gently said, 'it was brought there and jettisoned.'

'That's making it very hard,' Parfitt said. 'Unless chummie was carrying a hammer on board the half-decker, and went for his old man on Haynor Sounds.'

Gently smiled very slowly. 'We're getting ahead of the facts,' he said. 'Did French have any quarrel with the Speltons?'

'No quarrel we know of,' Parfitt said.

'Where else might he have been going?' Gently said.

Parfitt shook his head. 'Search me,' he said. 'Past the bungalows is Moorford Staithe, where there's two yards and a few more bungalows. Then you branch left for Haynor Sounds and Hickstead Broad and Marsey. Keep straight on for Sotherton. That's what's upstream from here.'

'Nearer than that,' Gently said.

'Well,' Parfitt said, 'what you can see. Just the bungalows, which are mostly let. We could get a list of residents from the post office.'

Gently took out his pipe, filled it, lit it. He leaned elbows on the parapet and stared. Reuben's Cakewalk was thundering 'Valencia', a tall gaff sail was inching downstream.

'Get on to the River Police,' Gently said. 'Try to find some of the other craft that moored here on Tuesday. In fact, we know nothing except that French left his office at ten, and that you think the son is lying.'

'And that he collects,' Parfitt said.

'Yes,' Gently said. 'That too.'

CHAPTER THREE

A T FOUR FIFTY-FIVE a.m. on Friday August 7th a milk
float clattered over Haynor Bridge and the driver,
looking to his left, saw a bulky man in a tweed jacket
unpopping the canvas cover of a white-painted launch.
The launch was conservative in design, but its lines were
conserving something very beautiful and on the lotus-
blossom shape of its transom appeared: *WHITE
HERON Haynor Country Club*, in flowing copperplate,
gilt, shadowed. The man heard the float and
straightened to look at it. His eyes met the eyes of the
driver. His eyes were greenish-hazel eyes which had a
mild expression but which were nevertheless penetrat-
ing. The driver didn't know who this man was but
supposed he might be a doctor or perhaps a medical
specialist on holiday. The expression of his eyes startled
the driver and the driver remembered it for some time
afterwards. Later he saw a newspaper picture of the man.
He was Superintendent George Herbert Gently.

The milk float went. Then it was very quiet again.
Though there was no breeze a whitish mist was twisting

and driving along the river. Reuben's fair stood still and sheeted. Wet-awninged yachts lay still along the quays. The bridge, carrying five hundred years, lay wetly still. The surface of the water lay like lightly smoked glass. Gently folded the cover, stowed it, went ashore for the painters, coiled the painters on the planked decks, fore and aft, stepped back into the launch. His movements in the launch rippled the water which just there was blued with oil, and from that and from the launch rose a cold smell of petrol and smell of river which was the smell of waterlilies. He felt in a side-locker, took out a cloth, ran it over the cream leather upholstery of the driver's seat. He sat, switched on, closed the choke. He pressed the starter. The launch trembled.

When he drove out from the Club moorings the sun had reached the top of French's office building and the white paint on which the sign was painted showed reddish-lemon in a pale sky. He drove at the launch's slowest speed, turned upstream, below the bridge. The vault of the bridge had yellow scores and reflected the throb of the engine as a rumble. French's wet boathouse showed dark timber beams, wash sounded hollowly up the Spelton slipways. The metal furniture on the Bridge Inn lawn streamed with dew above dew-sodden grass. The launch pressed softly over the weak ebb. Its wash veed out from bank to bank. When the wash of the launch reached a moored craft the craft heaved slightly and was still again. In front of the launch the water was luminous. Behind the launch the water was grey.

He drove past the sheds, past the rond moorings, past an old boat upturned on the bank, past the houseboat converted from a ship's lifeboat, into the bungalowland of fretted quays. The bungalows had names such as Osokosi, R EEEE, Dutch Hutch and La Cabina, and occasionally names such as Uprond and Marshways and Heronby. They were of timber with tin roofs or roofs of coloured felt tile. They were small, single-storeyed, and brightly but ineptly painted. A few had been factory-designed or followed some structural scheme but the majority resembled a collection of outhouses which had grown to fill the available space. They were old. The plots they occupied were only as deep as the river rond. A little scurfy grass in front of each one of them ended in decayed piling of non-professional origin. Short shallow boat-dykes held a few small craft and collected scum and flotsam from the river. Some baroque decoration of paint-thickened timber invested an occasional veranda or gable-end. They were old. They had outside closets. Water would need to be carried to them. Tolofin. Kumfee.

Gently continued to drive very slowly, his gaze shifting from bank to bank. The bungalows were placed so near one another that the marshes behind them were mostly hidden. The marshes were below the level of the river and the bungalows made their own skyline and the sun, brilliant but still reddish, lay on the roofs to the left. The stream bore east. Moorford church lay to the east. Its grey tower, the buttresses battered, rode a green slope a mile distant. On the left bank a windpump tower stood rusty brown in full sun, and at that point the bungalows ended and the banks were reeded down both sides. Tall reeds, pastel green, left whispering as the launch passed them. Full of tiny grey-brown birds who poured out rusty creaking song. Gently went on driving. He passed Moorford Staithe. It had a small yard, a few more bungalows, a ferry pontoon niched into the bank. A branch of the stream turned left and the branch was signposted: Hickstead & Marsey. Ahead, very distant over the marshes, appeared the cream-white breasts of the coastal sandhills. Behind the sandhills was hyacinth blue. Here it was that Gently turned the launch.

William Archer was a thin man. 'No,' he said. 'I don't believe it.' He kept shaking his head and staring at the skirting and sucking his breath through his lips. 'No,' he said. 'Not that.' He had a pendulous nose and it was bluish.

'How long have you been here?' Gently said.

'Seven, eight years,' Archer said. 'Harry advertised the post. I knew him. We used to come here for holidays. I was on a yard down at Maldon. I'm a foreigner all right. I dare say that's why Harry picked me. They don't respect you unless you're a foreigner. You know how it is round here.'

'Have you any interest in the firm?' Gently said.

'No,' Archer said. 'No interest.'

'How much are you getting?' Gently said.

'Twenty-five hundred,' Archer said.

'It's a responsible job you have here,' Gently said.

'I'm getting paid for it,' Archer said. 'Twenty-five hundred is a pretty good screw. Ask some of the other managers what they're getting.' He looked at Gently, looked at the skirting. He had a long face with drooped lines. The skin was flaccid and the complexion flushed. They were sitting in his office with one of the blinds drawn. 'Of course, there's some perks,' Archer said. 'There's always something goes with the job. Like my motor-cruiser, I get that maintained, and anything I need doing to my house. I never quarrelled with Harry about that. There's plenty would like to walk in here.'

'So what did you quarrel with him about?' Gently said.

'Who's been saying I quarrelled with him?' Archer said. 'I may have had words with him once or twice. You didn't always know how to take Harry.'

'Words about what?' Gently said.

'About running the yard,' Archer said.

'Such as?' Gently said.

'Oh any mortal bloody thing,' Archer said. His hand went to the deep drawer of the desk, came away. He lit a cigarette clumsily. He took several quick puffs from the cigarette, looked at it. 'I got on with Harry all right,' he said. 'You're bound to have a set-to every now and then. He's got his way, you've got yours. They don't always click. You can't expect it. But we got on all right together, don't try to make anything out of that.'

'When was the last time you had words with him?' Gently said.

'Oh,' Archer said. He flicked the cigarette. 'I don't know, I can't remember,' he said.

'Wasn't it as late as last Tuesday?' Gently said.

'Last Tuesday?' Archer said, looking at Gently. He had yellowish-brown eyes and they were watering. 'Have you been talking to that girl in there?' he said.

44

'We talk to a lot of people,' Gently said.

Archer puffed at the cigarette.

'Tell me what happened on Tuesday,' Gently said. 'A man gets murdered. Something has to lead up to it. Tuesday wasn't just another day. What happened on Tuesday?'

'What are you getting at?' Archer said. 'I didn't have anything to do with it. I was in the pub over there. You know I was. You've been asking people.'

'Of course,' Gently said. 'They remember you were in there. But they weren't with you after you came out. You drove home, you say. Alone.'

'But I did,' Archer said. 'My wife told you. I was in by eleven. This is bloody mad, that's what it is.'

'Yes,' Gently said. 'What happened on Tuesday?'

Archer stared at nothing in particular. His thin lips sagged at the corners. His hand went to the deep drawer again, opened it, groped, came out with a Vat 69 bottle. He groped again, found a tumbler, spilled whisky into it. He didn't watch his hands do this. When the whisky was poured he drank it.

'I know it looks bad,' he said. 'Me having a row with Harry, all that. I know the way you look at things. Somebody hit him over the head.'

'What was the row about?' Gently said.

'Have a drink,' Archer said. 'No, all right, I know you won't. Maybe you're not a drinking man.'

He poured some more whisky and drank it.

'I wasn't a drinking man,' he said. 'A couple of bitters, that was me. Point of fact, I didn't like it. You know, it was only by chance I went down to the pub. The girls had gone to a show in Starmouth and the missus was out at her sister's. Another night I wouldn't have gone, that's just the way things happen. So first you think it was young French who did it. Now you think it was me.'

'It could have been you,' Gently said.

'Now I'm drowning it in booze,' Archer said. 'Only I was drowning it in booze before then, and never hit Harry over the head. I'm not drunk either. You can tell it by the bottle. I had a nip at home, that's all.'

'Harry came in here to talk to you,' Gently said.

'All right,' Archer said, 'why ask me? That fluffy bitch in the next room has probably got it down in shorthand. Not that it's new, any of it. She'll know it off by heart by now.'

'He didn't like you drinking,' Gently said.

'To hell with my drinking,' Archer said. He picked up the bottle with a sort of flourish, poured whisky, drank it. 'Rows,' he said. 'What are they always about? Bloody money, that's what. Don't let the set-up here fool you. We've lost thousands on one or two contracts.'

'And French blamed you?' Gently said.

'Aren't I his manager?' Archer said. 'It's all my fault that wages go up and timber and every damned thing else. And I warned him about it, that was my fault. I told him his estimating was crazy. And I was right, that's what really needled him. Harry thought he couldn't make a mistake.'

'And yet you say you got on with him,' Gently said.

Archer gestured with the tumbler. 'That's not a lie, either. When things went right I got on with Harry, I knew how he worked. He was vain as the devil. That's why he couldn't take it when things didn't go right – he was losing face, you know how they are. So he'd come in here and take it out on me. And then I'd take it out on a bottle.'

'And it was like that Tuesday,' Gently said.

'Yes,' Archer said. 'Just like that. He'd seen the worksheets of a job we've contracted and it'll be a loss and he blew his top. Mind you, he was niggly before that. One of the yachts came in smashed up. A *Nereid* copped it with its bowsprit, stove in a couple of yards of coaming. You're getting damage all the time, the Broads are jampacked with hire-boats. But Harry got upset about it. He was in one of his black moods.'

'You mean before that happened?' Gently said.

'Right from the start,' Archer said. 'I reckoned he'd had a spat with his son. They both turned up looking like death.'

'What was the son doing all day?' Gently said.

'Loafing,' Archer said, 'loafing around. You can drive your son into the yard, but you can't make him work. The son likes to go sailing. He doesn't like scrubbing bottoms.'

'Were they rowing at the yard?' Gently said.

'No,' Archer said, 'I don't think so.'

'Did they go home to lunch?'

'Harry did,' Archer said. 'I saw young French having his in the restaurant.'

'Did they go home to tea together?'

'I shouldn't think so,' Archer said. 'Harry took off in a huff after he'd chewed me up, and if young French was going sailing he'd have had his tea here. But don't ask me, I wasn't checking up. I finished the bottle and went home.'

He poured more whisky into the tumbler. He sipped a little, didn't finish it. The corners of his mouth were still pulled. He looked up from under his brows at Gently.

'All right,' he said. 'French didn't like it. Told me to knock it off or he'd sack me. Harry was always threatening to sack people, that was one of his little ways.'

'On Tuesday?' Gently said.

'Not only on Tuesday,' Archer said.

'But especially on Tuesday,' Gently said.

Archer sipped some more whisky.

'Now you've got a motive,' he said. 'Opportunity, motive. But just the same it's bloody crazy, because Harry wouldn't have sacked me. And how did I know where to find him, how did I know he was coming back to the office?'

'That's a question, isn't it?' Gently said. 'Do you think someone might have phoned him?'

Archer drank. 'You're a clever bastard,' he said. 'Did you phone him?' Gently said.

'I didn't phone him I didn't see him I didn't hit him,' Archer said. 'Look, I don't go about killing people. I'm not the sort who goes about killing people. I never even thought of killing anyone. All I do is hit the bottle. I hit it on Tuesday and kept on hitting it. Try to get me for drunken driving.'

'But somebody did kill him,' Gently said.

'If you want my idea, they didn't,' Archer said. 'Not

meaning to kill him, not like that. Not going after him to do him in.'

'Then how was it done?' Gently said.

Archer finished the whisky, poured some more. 'Don't think you've got me drunk,' he said. 'This stuff is mother's milk to me.'

'So how was it done?' Gently said.

'It's up to you to find out, isn't it?' Archer said. 'I don't know who did it. I've thought about it. I don't know of anybody who'd try to do for Harry. They might have said they would, but they wouldn't, at the pinch. His son wouldn't have done it. Murder's rare in these parts.'

'So,' Gently said.

'It was an accident,' Archer said. He swilled the whisky around in his glass, watched it swilling while he spoke. 'Harry was in one of his moods. He was a bastard when he was moody. Acted like people were muck, like his shit didn't stink. And he was handing it to someone who couldn't take it, who'd maybe had too much of Harry. And they let fly at him. And he went in. And they cast off the launch to try to cover up a bit. I'm bloody certain that's the way it happened, it's the only way that makes sense.'

Gently said: 'They let fly at him.'

Archer drank. 'Yes,' he said.

'They were provoked, so they hit him,' Gently said.

Archer just watched the whisky.

'With a weapon,' Gently said.

'You think it was a hammer,' Archer said.

'Do you think it was a hammer?' Gently said.

49

'If you don't know, I can't tell you,' Archer said. He flicked a look at Gently that didn't quite focus, dropped his eyes to the tumbler again. 'They might've been fighting,' he said. 'Harry was a big man to fight with. Maybe they picked up a hammer to keep him off, and Harry wouldn't keep off.'

'There was a hammer handy on the river bank?'

'Perhaps they were doing a job,' Archer said.

'Late at night in the dark?' Gently said.

'Or,' Archer said, 'it mightn't have been a hammer.'

'Not a hammer,' Gently said.

Archer emptied the glass, smacked it down on the desk. 'By Christ, I thought Harry was a bastard,' he said to the tumbler. 'Why me? Why am I landed in this shit?'

'What was French doing back at the office that evening?' Gently said.

'Checking the books,' Archer said. 'I was swindling him, didn't you know? How should I know why he came back to the office, I was over the bridge, I was drinking my supper.'

'Could he have been looking for his son?' Gently said.

'Yes, blame the son,' Archer said. 'Why should I stand up for him, anyway? I'm no pals with young French, he skulks around like a pain in the neck. His father rowed him. Good motive. Do your Ogpu act with him.'

'I'm told he was running after a woman,' Gently said.

Archer went quite still, said nothing.

'You know about that?' Gently said.

'Nobody told me,' Archer said.

'With,' Gently said, 'a woman of reputation. The wife of one of your yard-hands. Lidney.'

'She's got a reputation all right,' Archer said. 'Sid's missus. Sid don't care.'

'But Harry French might have cared,' Gently said.

Archer shook his head, staring at the tumbler.

'I'm told he would have done,' Gently said.

'He wouldn't have known, anyway,' Archer said. 'Nobody told Harry any gossip. I didn't hear about it. He wouldn't have done. And if he'd heard he wouldn't have cared. It was coming into the business he rowed young French about.'

'Suppose someone told him,' Gently said.

Archer shook his head, drew breath through his lips. 'Probably nothing in it anyway, just gossip,' he said. 'Harry wouldn't have got stewed up about that.'

Gently said: 'When French was missed you seemed to think he might have committed suicide. I'm told you searched the yard for him. What made you do that?'

'Oh,' Archer said. His eyes met Gently's again. 'I don't know,' he said. 'I got a feeling something was wrong. The way the office door wasn't locked. That wasn't like Harry. And he was human, he'd been fretting, ever since his missus died. Sometimes I was even sorry for him. I got a feeling, that's all.'

'How hard did those contracts hit him?'

'He wasn't ruined,' Archer said. 'Nothing like that. The trouble was inside. A bottle or a woman might have fixed him.'

His eyes went past Gently to the window, the window where the blind wasn't drawn. Gently turned his head. A man stood squinting at the window. The man was humpty and wore dungarees. Archer half rose.

51

'That's Sid,' he said. 'He's got a new job. He'll be wanting instructions.'

'Sid Lidney?' Gently said.

'Yes, the one with the wife,' Archer said. 'I've made him in charge of boat's furniture.'

Gently looked at Lidney. Lidney turned away. Archer frowned.

'I'd better talk to young French,' Gently said. 'Is he at the yard today?'

'I'll have him fetched,' Archer said.

Gently said: 'Don't bother. I'll find him.'

Thus: Gently searched for John French in the dry boathouses and the wet boathouses; in the building shops, in the engineering shops, in the smith's shop, in the joiner's shop; in the rigger's shop, in the varnishing shop, in the boat's furniture and a number of other shops; in the timber store, in the paint store, in the fittings store and in the sail loft; in all which he took great interest, but in none of which he found John French. As he was leaving the reception office, where John French also was not, a Wolseley drove on to the cindered parking area and Parfitt got out.

'Morning sir,' Parfitt said.

'Morning,' Gently said. 'Drop the sir.'

'I've been talking to the River Police,' Parfitt said. 'I got on to them last night like you told me. They've turned up some witnesses at Harning, the people on *Vestella* 7. Name Clifford, come from Coventry, two couples and a kid.'

'What did they see?' Gently said.

'They saw Harry French,' Parfitt said. 'Anyway, they saw the launch leave and head upstream. They couldn't see who was in it, of course. They were moored opposite, further down, on a bit of soft rond round the corner. They'd been to the fair. They were just walking back. They'd let the kid stop at the fair till ten p.m. They'd been up Hickstead way all the weekend and had just come down on the Tuesday. Hard evidence. It all clicks.'

'Coming to the evidence,' Gently said.

'Yes,' Parfitt said, 'all five of them saw it. The old boy Clifford is a regular Broadsgoer and hot about the rules of navigation. So he sees this launch without any lights creeping away from French's quay, and he has a bind about it to the others, and they all take notice. A varnished or dark-painted launch around eighteen feet long. No lights. Just the driver. Going up very quietly through the bridge. The River Police have taken the statements. The Cliffords are handing over tomorrow. They're making their way back to Hofton; we can pick them up with a launch if you like.'

'Have you brought the statements?' Gently said.

'They're coming,' Parfitt said. 'I had the info on the phone. The patrol rang us from Harning.'

'I'll see the statements,' Gently said. 'Doesn't sound as though much can be added to them. But they're a break all right. We're beginning to know where we are.'

'Me, I was out of my depth,' Parfitt said. 'That's about where I was. And the body found up there too, as though the facts weren't clear enough.'

'In Speltons' slipway,' Gently said. 'When the bank up that way is fretted with cuttings.'

Parfitt looked at him. 'Christ, yes,' he said. 'I don't know what I've been using for brains. All those cuts are flotsam traps. The body couldn't have got far from where it went in.'

'And it fetched up in the lowest of them,' Gently said. 'Except for French's half-decker boathouse.'

'Speltons' quay,' Parfitt said.

'There or somewhere just above it,' Gently said.

Parfitt stared hard at Gently.

'I want you to take the Club launch,' Gently said. '*White Heron*, she's moored by the bridge, I've got the use of her while I'm here. Take her up through the bridge and prowl along both banks. See what you can find, witnesses, indications. Tomorrow is hand-over day. We haven't a lot of time to do it.'

'I'll handle it,' Parfitt said. 'I've brought Joyce with me. He can do some leg work.'

'Send him higher up,' Gently said. 'We're not so sure of ourselves yet. But you stick to the first two hundred yards. I've a feeling it was somewhere there.'

'Me too,' Parfitt said. 'Have you had any luck here, sir?'

'Drop the sir,' Gently said. 'I've been watching the manager drink whisky. Now I want to talk to the son, but I don't seem able to ferret him out.'

'Have you tried the *Kiama*?' Parfitt said.

'No,' Gently said. 'What's the *Kiama*?'

Parfitt turned, pointed to a plot of land which lay behind the building shops. A long black yacht-hull stood on the plot, shored up with oil drums and timber packing. It had a straight stem and a counter stern and there was carving on the counter which had traces of gilding. A very long bowsprit projected over its stem. The oil drums were nested in a bed of nettles.

'That's the *Kiama*,' Parfitt said. 'She was a famous boat in my father's day. Now she's pulled out there to rot and all the yard-hands do their scrounging on her.'

'What's the matter with her?' Gently said.

'Damn all, probably,' Parfitt said. 'But all the big yachts like her are finished. No room any more. Listen behind you.'

From behind them, from the river, came the surges of many engines and the wash of turbulent water and the creak of boats at moorings.

The *Kiama* had a delicate sheer line and her bilge was turned like a woman's cheek.

Gently went over to the *Kiama*, climbed the ladder which lay against her counter. From the ladder he stepped on to a planked deck and from the deck over a coaming into her well. The saloon doors stood open and her big hatch was pushed back and in the saloon a young man was standing with a closed book in one hand. The young man had brown eyes and the brown eyes were fixed on Gently. The brown eyes were close together and the face and the skull were both narrow. The head was set flush on the shoulders with a very short neck and the head was highest at the back and the ears were large though flat. The nose was large. The complexion was fresh. The mouth was handsome but small. The chin was small also. The young man had good shoulders. He was wearing a coffee-coloured sports shirt and dark brown slacks and Magister yacht shoes and a gold wristwatch. The book was Thomas Carew's *Poems*. He was holding it with a finger in his place. He said:

'Who are you – what are you after?'

'Superintendent Gently, C.I.D.,' Gently said. He stepped down into the saloon, stood leaning in the hatchway. The saloon of the *Kiama* had less than full standing headroom. 'You're John French,' Gently said.

'All right, suppose I am,' John French said. 'What do you want now?'

'Just to talk to you,' Gently said. 'Sit down again. This place will do. It'll probably do better than the office.'

John French hesitated, sat. His large ears had become red. He sat on one of the wide settee-berths which ran down each side of the *Kiama's* saloon. Each of the settee-berths was a double and at the end of each was a large sideboard locker and because the berths were so wide they were equipped with settee-backs which slotted into the lockers and the after bulkhead. The saloon coamings had oval windows with sliding panes and faded rep curtains. The bulkheads and lockers were of panelled mahogany and the coamings were of plain mahogany. The roof and its beams were white-enamelled. Brass oil lamps were gimballed over the lockers. A drop-leaf mahogany table furnished the cabin sole which was covered with buff lino protected by brass strip. Gently sat on the settee-berth opposite to John French. It was very warm in the saloon of the *Kiama*.

'What – why do you want to talk to me?' John French said.

'I've read your statement,' Gently said.

56

John French looked at the book, which he'd closed up. 'What about my statement?' he said.

'It's not too convincing,' Gently said. 'And it leaves out one or two matters that interest us. Like how you managed to sail so far after the wind died on Tuesday. And what your conversation with your father was about over breakfast on that day. Perhaps some other small points.'

'There was plenty of wind on Tuesday,' John French said.

'Not according to Mr Willard,' Gently said. 'He's your county meteorologist. He recorded a light variable southerly airstream until the early afternoon, then a similar north-easterly sea breeze which faded out during the evening.'

'You can't go on that stiff,' John French said.

'It seems reasonably authentic,' Gently said.

'You wouldn't sail at all if you depended on that,' John French said. 'There was some wind. I had enough.'

'Was it north-easterly?' Gently said.

'Well, I suppose so,' John French said. 'If they say that's where it came from I shan't call them liars.'

'Right,' Gently said. 'So you'd be tacking. Tacking over the tide to Hickstead Staithe. Against a fading variable breeze. A distance of five and a half miles. You say you started out at six-thirty. What was the time when you got to Hickstead?'

'I didn't go to Hickstead,' John French said.

'But you said you did in your statement,' Gently said.

'Not to Hickstead Staithe,' John French said. 'I didn't

say that in my statement. I know what I said. I said nearly to Hickstead Staithe. Actually, I turned round at the bottom of the broad. I didn't want to go down to that hole.'

'That would make it five and a quarter miles,' Gently said. 'Are you sure you didn't turn at the top of the broad?'

'I've just said the bottom,' John French said.

'Yes,' Gently said. 'So what was the time?'

John French twisted the book over.

'Were you wearing your watch?' Gently said.

John French hesitated. 'Yes,' he said. 'I was wearing my watch all right.'

'Then surely you looked at it?' Gently said. 'People out sailing usually check their times. Especially when they've reached where they intend to go and want to estimate how long it will take them to get back.'

'So what?' John French said. 'I didn't look at mine.'

'Perhaps you were watching the other boats,' Gently said.

'What other boats?' John French said.

'That very noisy red-and-cream speedboat,' Gently said. 'I understand it was making a nuisance of itself all the evening.'

John French twisted the book. 'I didn't notice,' he said. 'They're a lot of morons who have speedboats. I don't pay any attention to them.'

'But this one you'd have noticed,' Gently said. 'On a quiet broad you couldn't help it. Bellowing around like a stung cow. Chivvying other boats. Getting shouted at. Perhaps you shouted at it yourself?'

'I don't pay any attention to them,' John French said.

'And you sailed slowly down the broad and back without noticing it?'

'I,' John French said. 'Yes. I didn't notice it.'

'Whether it was there or wasn't there?' Gently said.

'Yes. It wasn't there,' John French said.

'I see,' Gently said. 'But you guessed wrongly. I didn't make that boat up. The driver's name was Oswald Blifil. He's being summonsed. You weren't at Hickstead.'

'I,' John French said. 'All right, I did see him. I was only putting it on when I said I didn't.'

'You saw Oswald Blifil?'

'I don't know about that,' John French said. 'I saw a red-and-cream speedboat, I don't know who was driving it.'

'But you saw the red-and-cream speedboat.'

'Yes,' John French said.

'Odd,' Gently said. 'That's the part I made up. Blifil's speedboat is royal blue.'

John French didn't say anything. He sat still, eyes lowered. The flush had extended from his ears to his cheeks and his lips were dry and slightly parted. He had tight hold of Thomas Carew's *Poems*.

'You were lying,' Gently said. 'You didn't go for a sail in a half-decker. That story won't stand up for a moment, we can trap you all along the line. You couldn't have got to Hickstead in the time. You don't know what happened at Hickstead that evening. You can't produce a witness who saw you there or on the way there, going or coming. You have given a false account of your movements from early evening till midnight on Tuesday.'

John French didn't say anything.

'So where were you?' Gently said.

'I was where I said I was,' John French said. 'I can't help about speedboats. It's like I told you, I don't notice them.'

'And you can't help about the wind?' Gently said.

'You can't prove there wasn't enough wind,' John French said. 'I don't need much. I can sail. You can't prove I didn't go to Hickstead and back.'

Gently said: 'Let's put it another way. This is a very serious matter. We know you didn't get on with your father and that there was persistent trouble between you. Your father was killed. You will have to give an account of your movements at the time he was killed in court. The story you have told us won't be believed. If you know of a better one, you'd better tell it.'

John French didn't say anything.

'Have I made it plain?' Gently said.

'I know you're against me,' John French said. 'Keep saying I'm lying when I'm telling the truth.'

'I'm not against you,' Gently said. 'I'm warning you. You won't be believed. And we'll get the truth of it, you can depend on that. You're a fool if you think you can lie your way out.'

'Prove I'm lying,' John French said. 'I don't care what you think.'

'It's what a jury thinks that matters. You may find yourself caring about that,' Gently said.

John French crouched a little on the settee-berth, let his head sink into his shoulders. The heat in the saloon of the *Kiama* was due to her having no awning rigged.

She smelled of dry timber and dry paint and sour upholstery and cigarette smoke, but she did not smell of rot. A tin on the table held many cigarette ends.

'Let's get back to Tuesday morning,' Gently said. 'What was the row about before you came to the yard?'

'What row?' John French said.

'You had a row with your father,' Gently said.

'Oh no I didn't,' John French said. 'You aren't going to talk me into that. We just had breakfast and came down here, that's all it was. There wasn't any row.'

'Perhaps about your working at the yard,' Gently said.

'You can perhaps all you like,' John French said. 'I'm not such a fool as you think I am.'

'Perhaps about Rhoda Lidney,' Gently said.

John French's head lifted. His eyes met Gently's. They stared into Gently's very hard. They were chocolate-brown eyes without streaks in them.

'Was she the trouble?' Gently said.

'Don't know what you're talking about,' John French said.

'About you and Rhoda Lidney,' Gently said. 'And about your father cutting up rough over it.'

John French kept meeting Gently's eyes. 'There's nothing about me and Mrs Lidney,' he said. 'He couldn't have cut up rough because there's nothing to know. And if anyone says there is they're liars.'

'So you don't even know Rhoda Lidney,' Gently said.

'I didn't say that,' John French said. 'I know her, all right. I know Sid. But that's not the same as the other thing.'

'You've been to their house,' Gently said.

'Not to do that I haven't,' John French said. 'I've been with Sid. There's nothing in that, is there? Sid and me get on together.'

'You're a friend of his?'

'Yes,' John French said, 'I suppose I'm allowed to have some friends. Sid taught me how to sail a boat. I haven't got many friends round here. And I've been up to his once or twice and we've gone fishing and babbing together. I've never been there except with Sid. It's all lies if they say I have.'

'We've been hearing lies, then,' Gently said. 'And perhaps your father heard them too.'

'I tell you he didn't,' John French said. 'There was nothing to hear and he wouldn't have cared anyway.'

All this time he was looking straight at Gently though his chin was sinking down to his chest.

'You might have been with Rhoda Lidney Tuesday night,' Gently said.

'I, I was out sailing,' John French said.

'Following a row about her in the morning,' Gently said.

'Don't I keep telling you there wasn't one?' John French said. 'You're making all this up, you think it's clever or something, but it's a lot of bull, that's what. You can't prove it. I've told the truth.'

'Where do the Lidneys live?' Gently said.

John French said nothing.

'Perhaps in the bungalows,' Gently said, 'upstream of the bridge?'

John French flung his book on the table. 'What's the

use of talking to you?' he said. 'You're going to blame it on to me somehow, that's all they've fetched you down here for. And it's a damn shame, that's what it is, you think I've no one to stand up for me. But I'm going to get a lawyer, my father's lawyer. I'm not going to be bullied around like this.'

'You might as well tell me,' Gently said, 'I can find out from the next yard-hand.'

'And why has it got to be me?' John French said. 'There's dozens of people had it in for my father.'

'Such as who?' Gently said.

'Dozens,' John French said. 'Nobody liked him. Dozens. Dozens! What about the Speltons – why aren't you going after them?'

'Why should I be?' Gently said.

'You don't even know,' John French said. 'And you don't care. You're just after me. Because I'm his son and come in for the money, that's the only reason, you can't prove anything. But I can tell you something, the Speltons stand to gain, they knew I'd sell to them like a shot. And Dave threatened to belt my old man. Just put that in your pipe and smoke it.'

John French panted, and sweat gleamed on his forehead. He was leaning forward and his chin was pushed out.

'I see,' Gently said. 'What is it you're going to sell them?'

'Why not go and ask them?' John French said. 'It'll make a change from bullying me. See how you get on with Dave Spelton.'

'Yes,' Gently said. 'But why are you lying?'

'I don't have to sit here like this,' John French said. 'I don't have to answer any of your questions. I can have a lawyer. I've got the money.'

'Do you think you're shielding someone?' Gently said.

'Just don't talk to me like that,' John French said. 'You can talk to my lawyer, that's what.'

'You seem to be in need of one,' Gently said.

He was sweating too. It was very hot. His trousers were clinging behind his knees. The sun was over the edge of the *Kiama's* hatchway and reaching his ankles and feet. He rose, stepped out into the well. In the well one felt a little breeze. From the well one saw the rise of the *Kiama's* sheer to the line of her out-thrusting bowsprit. The bowsprit stood proud above the nettles. The *Kiama* was very still.

CHAPTER FOUR

T HUS: SUPERINTENDENT GENTLY went across to the
Country Club and there changed his tweed jacket
for a fawn linen jacket which he had been providential
enough to pack. He also exchanged his shoes for strap
sandals and removed his tie and unbuttoned his shirt and
after inquiry went into the Bridge Stores where he
purchased a straw hat of Italian manufacture. Then he
returned to the Club and ordered an iced lemonade
shandy which he drank through two straws; but before
allowing the rather pretty waitress who brought it to
depart he asked her:

'Where do the Lidneys live, miss?'

'Oh, them,' the waitress said. 'They live up the cinder
path.' She nodded where it was.

'How far up?' Gently asked.

'Oh, just past Speltons,' the waitress said. 'Marshways,
that's the name of the bungalow. I wouldn't live up
there if you paid me.'

'I'm not going to pay you,' Gently said.

'Well,' the waitress said, 'it's a dump. Though I dare

say it suits some people, probably you've heard about the Lidneys.'

'About Mrs Lidney,' Gently said.

'I don't know I'm sure,' the waitress said. 'A man must be a drip to let his wife carry on like that. They say he just goes out when she's got a bloke there. I don't know. There may be something wrong with him.'

'Is it anyone in particular?' Gently said.

'Not from what one hears,' the waitress said.

'I heard young French had been round there,' Gently said.

'Oh, him,' the waitress said.

'So I heard,' Gently said.

'Well,' the waitress said, 'it might do him some good. You know his trouble. He sits here making eyes at us. Hasn't got the pluck to speak up. The way he was brought up, I don't know, I shouldn't be running him down when he's in trouble.'

'His father was strict with him?' Gently said.

'So they say,' the waitress said. 'I'd better go.'

Then Gently drank the iced lemonade shandy. He watched the waitress serving. She was rather pretty.

Gently went out, took the cinder path which ran past the back of Speltons' sheds. The back of Speltons' sheds had three various doors, but each was locked or bolted inside. However, a notice pointed across the path to the gate of a redbrick house with newly painted woodwork. The notice said: Spelton Bros. (Jack Spelton–David Spelton) All Enquiries At The House. Gently went through the gate to the house. The front door of the

66

house was standing ajar. Through it Gently saw a hall and stairs and a door lettered Office – Ring And Wait. He rang and waited. Time passed. He rang again, waited again. While he waited he noticed that the hall was laid with Turkey-carpet pattern lino and that the stairs were laid with blue velour carpet and the walls papered with fawn and green urn-patterned paper. He noticed also that the woodwork was painted broken white with peppermint green trim and he had leisure to examine a photograph of some yachts which hung facing the office in an elaborate fretwork frame. The name Spelton was worked into the fretwork along with bulrushes, a windpump and a heron. Then Gently rang the bell for some twenty seconds, after which he heard a soft movement at the top of the stairs. He looked up the stairs. A girl stood on the landing. She was leaning on the guard rail. She was staring at Gently. Gently said:

'Hullo, there.'

'Hullo,' the girl said. She didn't move. Her eyes seemed very large, stared at Gently without winking.

'Are you in charge here?' Gently said, nodding his head at the office.

'Oh yes, I'm in charge,' the girl said. 'I look after everything. I'm in charge.'

'Well, would you mind coming down?' Gently said.

The girl didn't move for some moments. Then she straightened herself suddenly, came gliding, almost dancing down the stairs. She was smiling brilliantly.

'Who are you?' she said.

'I'm a policeman,' Gently said. He returned the smile.

'Oh,' she said, 'you'll be wanting a boat. And we haven't got one left. What a pity.'

'I'm not after a boat,' Gently said.

'Yes,' the girl said. 'They're all out. We're Speltons, we're always booked right up. I'm extremely sorry. We've nothing for you.'

She smiled again. It was a flashing smile. She had large china-blue eyes and they were opened wide. She had curling golden-brown hair that fell loosely, nearly to her shoulders. She was wearing a flowered knee-length dress and white ankle socks and tennis shoes. But she wasn't a girl, Gently now saw. Her age would be nearer to thirty.

'Well,' Gently said. 'I'm glad to hear you're booked up.'

'Oh, that doesn't matter,' she said. 'You can come into the office. I don't mind. Only I can't let you have anything, of course. All the booking's done through Hookers, but you'd know that, wouldn't you, if you're a policeman.'

'What's your name?' Gently said.

'V,' she said. 'It stands for Vera. Miss Vera Spelton. Dave and Jackie call me V.'

She opened the door of the office, went gliding through, stood holding it. She had a slim, narrow-hipped figure with a slight bust, but well-rounded limbs. Her nose was blunt, a little snubbed, had freckles round the bridge. Her mouth was wide and smiling. She was tanned. She smelled of sunwarm hay. She pushed a chair towards Gently.

'Do sit down,' she said.

Gently sat. Vera Spelton skipped to a chair behind an old walnut writing-table. There were two other chairs in the office and a filing cabinet and a chest of drawers, and on the walls hung many photographs of yachts and each photograph was in a fretwork frame. In addition there was a fretwork case containing a stock of burgee-badges in the Spelton colours, and a fretwork holder of coloured yacht postcards and a fretwork perpetual calendar on the writing-table. Vera Spelton picked up the calendar, adjusted it, replaced it, smiled at it.

Now,' she said, 'about the yacht you're having. You can't have *Victor*. *Victor's* out. You can't have *Damsel*, *Tomboy* or *Maid* or any of the *Breezes*, they're all out. Then there's *Melody, Insignia, Eclipse, Flame, Ensign, Novice* and *Dolly*. Nothing there. Then there's the *Bird* class, one to six. Fully booked. You don't seem very lucky, do you?'

No,' Gently said. 'Perhaps some other time.'

'Oh, I'd fix you up if I could,' Vera Spelton said. 'Would you be one of our old customers?'

'Not so very old,' Gently said.

'I'm not old at all,' Vera Spelton said. 'Do you think I'm attractive? Do you like me?' She leaned across the table. 'I'll tell you a secret,' she said. 'Some of our customers think I'm attractive.'

'Some of your customers?'

'Shh,' Vera Spelton said. 'It's a secret. You mustn't let my brothers know. They're very angry if people think I'm attractive. Silly, isn't it? That's how they are.' She drew back, still smiling. 'In the boats,' she said. 'Some of them have kissed me and put their arms round me and

69

tried to do naughty things. I don't let them, of course. But they try. They think I'm attractive.'

'Why do you go in the boats with them?' Gently said.

'Oh,' she said, 'there's lot's of excuses. To see if they've got clean sheets or know about the toilet, any excuse to go in the cabin with them. Then my arm gets round their waist, that's one of the ways I'm attractive, or I touch them in a special way. It's very easy when you know how.'

'And your brothers are angry?' Gently said.

Vera Spelton pouted. 'They shout at me. They shout at the customers. That's not the way to run a business, is it?'

'I'm not a businessman,' Gently said.

'No,' Vera Spelton said. 'It's silly. But it makes it exciting, knowing they'll be angry. I don't mind them shouting at me.'

'I take it you're only attractive to the customers,' Gently said.

'Oh, I attract most people,' Vera Spelton said. 'Only I can't go into the boats with other people, you have to go somewhere with them alone.'

'How about somebody else's boat?' Gently said.

'No,' she said. 'Then I wouldn't have an excuse. It's very complicated, really it is. If you don't know the rules you can't do it.'

'Did you use to attract Mr French?' Gently said.

Vera Spelton's eyes smiled an inquiry. 'Who is that?' she said. 'I don't know who you mean.'

'Your neighbour,' Gently said. 'The man who kept the yard across the road.'

Vera Spelton shook her head. 'Don't go there for a boat,' she said. 'Their boats are no good, they're all rubbish. Nobody goes to them twice. Did you just want a boat for yourself, or is it a party you want it for?'

'You'll know his son, John French,' Gently said. 'Harry French the father, John French the son. French's boat-yard. Harry French. You'd have known Harry French?'

'I'm extremely sorry,' Vera Spelton said. 'All our boats are out in any case. We're Speltons, of course, we're always booked up. I don't think we can do anything for you.'

'Harry French,' Gently said, 'in his launch.'

'We don't cater for launch-hirers,' Vera Spelton said.

'A big man in a launch,' Gently said.

'We don't like launch-parties here,' Vera Spelton said. Suddenly she picked up the calendar, held it out to Gently. 'You didn't know I did fretwork, did you?' she said. 'I've done all this in here.'

'Harry French, who made your brothers angry,' Gently said.

'Yes, I'm very good at it,' Vera Spelton said. 'They won't let me work on the boats, though I'm just as clever as they are, so this is what I do. I could sell it for money if I wanted. Do you do fretwork?'

Gently said nothing.

'I really could sell it,' Vera Spelton said. 'All sorts of things. Even furniture. I'm just as clever as they are.'

She smiled at Gently without meeting his eyes, smiled at the calendar, the writing-table. A flashing smile. She had small brown hands with mobile, flat-tipped fingers.

The fingers moved about the calendar, feeling the outline of the design. She breathed quickly. The smile lighted every part of her sunned face. Gently's shoulders lifted.

'Where can I find your brothers?' he said.

'Oh,' she said. 'Dave and Jackie. I don't know. They're not here.'

'Aren't they in the yard?' Gently said.

'I couldn't say where they are,' she said. 'But it's no use going to them. I'm afraid you must come back some other week.'

Gently nodded. 'I'll be back,' he said. He rose, turned towards the door. He met a man coming in through the door. The man had approached the door on tiptoe.

The man was nearly as tall as Gently and he had angry yellowish-grey eyes. He had a hard, broad frame with flat shoulders and large but well-formed hands. He was in his late thirties. He had a small moustache. He had Vera Spelton's blunt nose. He had Vera Spelton's wide mouth, but without Vera Spelton's smile. His mouth and face and body were taut and his eyes were fastened on Gently's. He wore an old dragged tweed jacket and a faded red cotton shirt and dungaree trousers and ragged plimsolls. He went flat-footed very slowly. In a tight, low-pitched voice he said:

'What are you doing here?'

'Routine inquiries,' Gently said.

'Oh, and who are you supposed to be?' the man said. Gently told him.

'I get it,' the man said. 'Getting V on her own. Seeing

72

what you could make her spill. A copper. A screw. A human ferret.'

'Oh, don't take on, Dave,' Vera Spelton said. 'It's only a policeman about a boat. I've told him that our boats are always booked up and he's just going and he wasn't naughty. You shouldn't've come interfering.'

'V,' David Spelton said, 'go and set the table.'

'But I've set the table,' Vera Spelton said. 'I have really, you can go and look.'

'Well, get on with your fretwork,' David Spelton said. 'I want to talk to this gentleman alone. Maybe we've got a boat he can have, I'll see about it. You finish that wall-bracket.'

'No, we haven't any boats,' Vera Spelton said. 'He'll have to go to those people.'

'V, just do what I say,' David Spelton said.

'All right, Dave,' Vera Spelton said.

She rose, smiling at neither of them. She glided round her brother. She vanished. David Spelton closed the door, leaned on it.

'I don't know if there's a law against it,' he said. 'Getting a subnormal person on their own and trying to work on them in that filthy way. But I'm going to find out, you can depend on that. And if it's an offence, I'm going to prosecute you. You think you're fireproof because you're a policeman, but you bloody aren't fireproof. Not with my sister.'

'It isn't an offence,' Gently said. 'Murder is. Investigating it isn't.'

'And that covers every dirty little trick,' David Spelton said. 'That's your excuse when you're caught out.' He came away from the door, went round the writing-table, leaned on the chair-back, stared. 'I heard what you were getting at,' he said. 'I know how your putrid mind is working.'

'Congratulations,' Gently said.

'People like you make me sick,' David Spelton said. 'Harry French interfering with V. It takes a policeman to think up filth like that. And you get her alone and keep feeding her with it, trying to plant it in her mind. But she isn't as stupid as that, you know. She's got her way of protecting herself. Because it's a lie. A damned lie. The dirty lie of a dirty mind.'

'Is it off your chest?' Gently said.

'What's the point of talking to you,' David Spelton said. 'Of course you've got a skin like a plastic fendoff, you wouldn't be in your line of business if you hadn't.'

'I might think you're afraid of something,' Gently said.

'Oh of course, of course,' David Spelton said.

'I didn't know you had a sister before I came here,' Gently said. 'I came to see you. About something quite different.'

'And V just fell into your clutches,' David Spelton said.

'You weren't eavesdropping early enough,' Gently said. 'She told me some very interesting things which I didn't know enough to prompt her in. What kept you so long at the yard after you saw me try the doors?'

David Spelton stared, said nothing.

'And now you're puzzling me,' Gently said. 'Suppose you drop the moral indignation before I find it significant?'

74

'Oh, very clever,' David Spelton said.

'What were you afraid I should get out of her?' Gently said.

'You've a thing about me being afraid,' David Spelton said. 'I'm not afraid, not of people like you. Only of the injury you might do to my sister. And it's got to end here, you understand? You're not shoving that lie at her again. Hawk your filthy ideas around to other people, but let V alone. Or you'll have me to deal with.'

'Shouldn't you just have walked in here,' Gently said, 'if your motive was to protect your sister from me?'

'I mean what I'm saying,' David Spelton said. 'Your being a policeman isn't going to protect you.'

'Yet you waited to eavesdrop,' Gently said. 'Till our interview was over. As though you wanted to hear what I was going to ask her, which you wouldn't have done if you'd come straight in. And Harry French's body turned up in your slipway.'

'I'll forget myself in a minute,' David Spelton said.

'I think you've already forgotten yourself,' Gently said. 'Why were you going to knock Harry French down?'

The knuckles of David Spelton's hands paled over the carved wood of the chair-back. His stare was less steady. He drew the chair a little towards him. He said:

'You're trying to build a case against me, is that it?'

'Routine inquiries,' Gently said.

'You can't fix one against young French. Now you're trying me for size.'

'Just asking questions,' Gently said. 'Why does everyone assume we're after young French?'

'Well, I don't fit,' David Spelton said. 'You're cooking it up first to last. Harry French never had anything to do with V. We never saw Harry French round here. He wasn't welcome, you understand? We hate Harry French's guts in these parts. If he'd stepped over that threshold I'd have kicked his arse, that's how welcome Harry French was here. He never met V, he never talked to her, you're up the spout with the whole deal. And come to that, he didn't run after women. That's the only decent thing I know about him.'

'But you seem to have had something against him,' Gently said.

'Am I saying I didn't?' David Spelton said. 'I'm not afraid to admit I hated his guts. You can hate a man's guts without killing him.'

'It's sometimes a preliminary step,' Gently said.

'It probably was in this case,' David Spelton said. 'But I didn't kill him all the same for that, nor I'm not shedding tears because someone else did. I couldn't care less, that's my position. I'd rather forget Harry French ever existed. It's just a bloody nuisance he wound up in our slipway and brought you and all the other ferrets trading their muck here. And if that's the lot you can get out. I've better things to do than talking to you.'

'More profitable things, perhaps,' Gently said.

'A darned sight more profitable,' David Spelton said.

'Like arranging a purchase with John French,' Gently said. 'Now his father is out of the way and can't prevent it.'

The chair jumped. David Spelton let go of it. He came round the table, stood close to Gently. He had a puffiness about his eyes and a slight tremor. The eye-whites were bloodshot.

'Like that, is it?' he said. 'You're full of reasons why I should have killed him. If it wasn't the one it was the other, and you're going to make something stick.'

'Will it stick?' Gently said.

'You rotten louse,' David Spelton said. 'I wouldn't have your job for the Bank of England. I'd sooner scrub bottoms for a living.'

'Compliments aside,' Gently said.

'I ought to belt you,' David Spelton said.

'It's been tried,' Gently said. 'But it never seemed to help anybody.'

'Yes,' David Spelton said, 'I ought to belt you.'

'Look,' Gently said, 'this is getting us nowhere. You might stack up an assault charge for yourself, but I'll still want the answers to my questions. Cool off. It's doing you no good. You don't act it well enough. You've lost too much sleep.'

'I'd love to belt you,' David Spelton said.

He raised his fist. Suddenly, he was sprawled on the floor. 'I told you, you'd lost too much sleep,' Gently said. 'That one was free. Don't do it again.'

David Spelton got up off the floor, hesitated, didn't do it again. He looked at Gently several times. Then he got out a cigarette and lit it. He went over to the window, looked out of the window. People were passing on the cinder path. David Spelton blew a lot of smoke at the window. He turned his back to it, blew smoke at the floor.

'All right,' he said, 'I shouldn't have done that. It's true, I haven't had too much sleep. We're working overtime. A rush job. In the sheds. You can see it.'

'How long have you been working overtime?' Gently said.

'A fortnight,' David Spelton said, blowing smoke. 'It's double pay if you put the men on it. The price won't stand double pay.'

'So you'd be there on Tuesday night,' Gently said.

'Jackie and I,' David Spelton said.

'Till what time?' Gently said.

'Midnight,' David Spelton said, blowing smoke.

'All the time,' Gently said.

'All the time,' David Spelton said. 'V fetched us a Thermos and sandwiches before she went to bed. Round about nine or just after.'

'Did you step outside at all?' Gently said.

'Only to the toilet,' David Spelton said.

'Where's the toilet?' Gently said.

'Top end of the sheds. You can see it,' David Spelton said.

Gently looked out of the window, saw a separate timber structure in a fenced piece of ground attached to the sheds. Next to the fence was a small cut grown up with reeds and then rough rond on which lay a decaying boat. Then the first bungalow. Gently said:

'Do you remember seeing anything when you went to the toilet?'

'Such as what?' Dave Spelton said.

'Such as any activity on the river,' Gently said.

'Yes,' David Spelton said, 'twice likely. Why should I remember anything like that?' He blew smoke. 'I don't remember seeing anything,' he said. 'You can ask Jackie. He was out there too.'

'Something coming by late,' Gently said. 'Without lights. Wouldn't you have noticed it?'

'If I'd seen it,' David Spelton said. 'But I didn't see it. I can't help you.'

'You didn't see Harry French?' Gently said.

'No,' David Spelton said, blowing smoke.

'Harry French didn't call at your sheds?' Gently said.

'No,' David Spelton said, blowing smoke.

'I see,' Gently said. 'Well, let's hear some more about Harry French. Why you hated him, that sort of thing. Why you were going to belt him. What he wouldn't sell you.'

'I thought you knew it all,' David Spelton said. 'You wouldn't want to listen to the lies I'd tell you.'

'Lies or truth, I want to listen,' Gently said. 'A lie often has the truth in the shape of it.'

David Spelton smoked a little, made a motion with his head. 'Then we'd better go across to the sheds,' he said. 'Jackie can tell you why we loved French, you can believe Jackie, he's not a liar. Jackie's the honest one of the family. Comes of being the eldest son.'

'I'd sooner hear it from you,' Gently said.

'Oh, I'll add my lies,' David Spelton said.

He moved to the door, opened it. Vera Spelton stood smiling in the hall. David Spelton looked at her, jerked his head towards the stairs. Vera Spelton didn't do anything, made no acknowledgement.

'V,' David Spelton said, 'you won't get that wall-bracket finished.'

'Oh I'm tired of fretwork,' Vera Spelton said. 'I'm coming across to the sheds too.'

'Not this morning, V,' David Spelton said. 'We've got some business to clear up. It's dull, it won't interest you. Come this afternoon. We'll do some painting.'

Vera Spelton pouted. 'No,' she said. 'I want to do something on the yacht.'

'Well, we'll see about it,' David Spelton said. 'This afternoon. But stay in this morning.'

'Yes, Dave,' Vera Spelton said. She smiled again but didn't move.

'Well, run along then,' David Spelton said.

'Yes, Dave,' Vera Spelton said.

David Spelton nodded, turned, went out. Gently followed. Vera Spelton danced after them.

'V,' David Spelton said over his shoulder.

'Yes, Dave,' Vera Spelton said. 'Yes, Dave. Yes, Dave.'

She kept behind them. David Spelton was silent. He led the way to the door near the noticeboard. He knocked twice on the door. The door was opened by a youngster in a boilersuit. They went through it and into a wide but shallow shed. A seagoing yacht was being built in the shed. The yacht was planked up and had the coamings fitted and there was a light in her and men were working in her and her planking was painted with pink priming. Her counter overhung a wall bench at the back of the shed, her bows overhung a slipway at the front. Doors were closed across the slipway, but wash came up it from passing boats and the sound of the wash was greatly magnified by the hollowness of the shed.

The air in the shed was heated and motionless. It smelled of raw timber, varnish, tar and tobacco smoke. In the unvarnished mahogany coamings of the yacht were lines of countersunk brass screwheads and the screwheads were new and yellow and the mahogany very smooth. An electric hand-drill burred intermittently inside the yacht; accompanying the burr was the soft clash of a push screwdriver. David Spelton looked at Gently, said:

'She's an East Coast Restricted Class. Thirty-three feet long. If we built them sideways we could manage a thirty-six foot job and just about screw her into a slipway. Bigger than that we can't handle them. Not without rebuilding and sacrificing our quays.'

'So,' Gently said.

David Spelton laughed. 'You'll get the idea in a minute,' he said. 'We taught the Frenches their business here, too damn well we taught them.'

He went to the yacht. A ladder with padded rests leaned against her gunnel. David Spelton climbed the ladder, leaned over the coaming, said something. The sound of the electric hand-drill stopped, the light in the yacht was hidden for a moment. A capped head came out of the hatch, turned towards Gently, said something. David Spelton came down the ladder. A man in tan dungarees followed him.

'My brother Jackie,' David Spelton said. 'Sorry he isn't dressed for company.'

'Yes, I'm Jack Spelton,' the man said. 'What's all this worrying about now?'

David Spelton said: 'You'll soon find out. The Superintendent's just getting his spike in. Seems he's heard of our business relations with the firm next door. He wants you to tell him all about them.'

'Oh,' Jack Spelton said. 'What's that to him?'

'You'd better ask him,' David Spelton said.

'What's that to you?' Jack Spelton said to Gently. 'You're rare curious, aren't you, about our affairs?'

Gently looked at Jack Spelton. Jack Spelton was several years older than his brother. He had a pinched version of his brother's face and his nose was sharper and he squinted a little. He had slack cheeks with deep lines in them and the wrinkled forehead of a dyspepsia sufferer. He was leaner built than his brother and less tall. He had the beginning of a stoop. He had greyed hair. Gently said:

'Just some routine questions.'

'They're never anything else,' David Spelton said.

'We like to get our facts straight,' Gently said. 'And your quarrel with Harry French is one of the facts.'

'Sounds like nosiness to me,' Jack Spelton said. 'We don't know anything about Harry French. Except I pulled him out of the bottom slipway and stuck him in the rigger's shop to drain. You know that, what more do you want?'

'You've heard what I want,' Gently said.

'Well, I don't like getting pulled off a job,' Jack Spelton said. 'There's too much of it going on. We've got work, some of us.'

He squinted at Gently, pulled a pipe out of his pocket, stuck it in his mouth, didn't light it. He drew on the pipe several times. He took it out of his mouth again, smacked his lips.

'All right then,' he said. 'It was over the Blackwater contract. Now you're as wise as you were before.'

'Don't tell him any lies,' David Spelton said. 'He's got a nose for lies like you have for rot.'

'Shut your trap, Dave,' Jack Spelton said. 'If you want me to tell the tale then keep out of it. It was in fifty-six or fifty-seven, the time they had the first Boat Show.'

'Go on,' Gently said.

'The first Boat Show,' Jack Spelton said. 'Cowells of Burnham were showing a yawl, a smart ocean-racing job. Forty-seven-six long, ten-nine, six-three, Columbian pine on oak frames, a bit narrow by our standards. I know Paul Cowell, met him during the war, he was up this way on an Admiralty contract. He booked a lot of orders for the yawl during the show, American mostly. More than he could cope with. So he got on to us to build him five, so be we could get them under the bridge. We reckoned we could do that all right on a low spring. All we had to do was to find room to build them.'

'And we didn't have to look far,' David Spelton said.

'Just keep quiet, Dave,' Jack Spelton said. 'If you'll step over to that window,' he said to Gently, 'you'll see where we could've built the Blackwater yawls.'

Gently stepped over to the window. From the window one looked at the house and the marshes to the right of it. But between the house and the marshes there lay a strip of meadow, neglected, partly overrun with brambles and elders. The meadow faced the rond adjacent to the sheds. It was separated only by the cinder path and by a dyke.

'That's it,' Jack Spelton said. 'Clay foundations. Doesn't flood. We've got planning permission, what's more, we went into it years back. That's the only place we can do anything. We mustn't build on the rond any more. But we can put in a slipway and launch over the path and that's all we need to build boats over there. And then we could build jobs of any size, provided they'd go through the bridge afterwards.'

'Just one thing only,' David Spelton said. 'We don't happen to own that bit of ground. And the late owner wouldn't sell us that bit of ground. And he pinched the Blackwater contract himself.'

'Dave,' Jack Spelton said, 'you'll make me angry. If you've got any sense you'll pipe down. It was only business. French didn't have to sell it. You seem to forget he was a competitor of ours.'

'I'm not forgetting,' Dave Spelton said. 'Dirty tricks like that I don't forget.'

'It was business,' Jack Spelton said. 'Harry could've played ball, but he didn't have to. I'm not saying I liked him the better for it, but he was inside his rights, he didn't owe us that land.'

David Spelton turned his back on his brother.

'Don't pay any attention to Dave,' Jack Spelton said. He raised his cap and scratched beneath it, squinted at Gently. 'Dave's touchy,' he said.

'How much was the contract worth?' Gently said.

'Oh, I don't know,' Jack Spelton said. 'We never got down to the brass tacks. I hear that Frenches lost money on it . . .'

'It was worth putting up a shed for,' Gently said.

'Well,' Jack Spelton said, 'we'd have had that after-wards, wouldn't we.'

'What did they sell at,' Gently said. 'Seven thousand, eight thousand – something like that?'

David Spelton said over his shoulder: 'We were aiming to clear ten thousand on it.'

'No, no, that's ridiculous,' Jack Spelton said. 'Might have been a couple of thou in it if we were lucky. Might have lost money, you can't tell. Could've been that Harry did us a favour.'

'Yes, he was the one for that,' David Spelton said.

'It's all a gamble these days,' Jack Spelton said. 'Every-thing going up, materials, labour. You have to blow boats together if you want to make any money.'

'Like hell,' David Spelton said. 'We'd have cleared that ten thousand.'

Jack Spelton stuck his pipe in his mouth, clenched his teeth over it hard.

All this while Vera Spelton had been gliding and dancing about the three men.

'So after that you wouldn't have had much personal contact with French,' Gently said.

Jack Spelton sucked. 'Never did have,' he said. 'He went about his business, we went about ours. I never went out of my way to have words with Harry French.'

'He didn't visit you at all?' Gently said.

'Why should he?' Jack Spelton said.

'You didn't see him about here?' Gently said.

'Unless he went by in his launch,' Jack Spelton said.

'He wasn't friends, say, with your sister?'

'Don't think she ever met him,' Jack Spelton said.

'Mind you don't lie,' David Spelton said.

Jack Spelton squinted at his brother's back.

'But you knew the son, of course, didn't you?' Gently said.

Jack Spelton sucked. 'That's different,' he said. 'We don't have any quarrel with young John. His old man and him are two different people.'

'You saw him about here quite a bit?'

'He's always welcome,' Jack Spelton said.

'You get on with him, do you?' Gently said.

'Well, yes,' Jack Spelton said. 'I don't have anything against him.'

'Oh for God's sake,' David Spelton said, turning, 'stop puzzling Jackie with your bloody cleverness. Just ask him straight, he can't tell you a lie. He'll only skate round the angles. Yes, John French did tell us he'd part with that land. Yes, we did know it long before Tuesday. No, John French wasn't hanging round V. No, we weren't trying to palm her off on him. All straight answers. Just ask straight questions. We don't care enough about you to lie.'

'Dave,' Jack Spelton said, 'have you gone right off your nut?'

'He makes me spew,' David Spelton said.

'I'm beginning to wonder,' Jack Spelton said. 'If you can't lay off you'd better get to hell out of it. The man's only doing his job, after all.'

'And what a job,' David Spelton said.

'That's about enough from you, Dave,' Jack Spelton said. 'Harry French got knocked on the head, you don't think they can just let it pass, do you? Somebody's got to come here looking into it, they can't let that sort of thing go on. And he's got to make a job of it, and find things out. He wants to nail the right bloke if he's going to nail anyone.'

'That's Jackie for you,' David Spelton said. 'He'd sooner have you hang him than think him unfair.'

'Your temper'll hang you yet,' Jack Spelton said. 'Take a reef in your tongue. Let the man ask his questions.' He looked towards Gently without meeting Gently's eye. 'Dave was spoiled by his mother,' he said. 'He still hasn't grown up.'

'I was spoiled by something,' David Spelton said.

'Dave,' Jack Spelton said.

David Spelton said nothing.

'All right then,' Jack Spelton said. 'There was some talk at the time with young John. He did give us to understand he'd sell us that piece when the time came. But I didn't pay much attention to it, you know the way these youngsters talk. Wait and see how he feels about it now he can do what he likes. Reckon he may think a bit different, a bit more like his old man. Anyway, I wasn't banking on it, and Dave didn't talk as though he was.'

'He's going to sell it to us,' David Spelton said.

'I don't know nothing about the other,' Jack Spelton said. 'I think that's squit. I've never seen anything of it. V's a good girl. She runs the house for us. We look after her, she looks after us. That's the way it's always been.'

'But I'm attractive,' Vera Spelton said, behind Gently.

'You're a good girl, V,' Jack Spelton said. 'You're a pretty mawther. You're all right.'

87

'Yes, I'm all right,' Vera Spelton said.

'So there's only one more question,' David Spelton said. 'Was it one or both of us who did for Harry French? Only we won't tell you, so of course you won't ask us, even Jackie could manage a lie about that.'

'Dave,' Jack Spelton said. He stopped. A face was peering through the window. The face belonged to Inspector Parfitt, it was frowning tightly to see into the shed. Gently moved to the door, opened it, looked out. Parfitt came along the path. He said quietly to Gently:

'We've found something sir. I'd like you to step round the corner for a moment.'

'Hmn,' Gently said. He looked back into the shed. Nobody moved, said anything. He shrugged, closed the door. Parfitt turned quickly to lead up the path.

'Nearly missed this one sir,' he said. 'Just by luck it caught my eye. I was tooling along very slow and I noticed the colour, and it clicked.'

'Colour of what?' Gently said.

'A strand of nylon,' Parfitt said. 'I left Joyce here on guard while I went back to the yard to check.'

He turned smartly on to the stretch of rough rond which lay between the Spelton yard and the first bungalow. A young slim fresh-faced man stood on the rond by the water's edge. Parfitt marched across to him. 'Here,' he said pointing downwards. Gently looked. He saw a rotted pile which was trussed to the bank by a steel rod. The head of the rod had a square plate under it and the wood had rotted from the plate and the plate had rusted sharp. In the crevice between the sharpened plate and the rotted wood was snagged an orange strand about an inch in length. Parfitt took from his pocket a coil of thin twisted orange nylon, one end whipped, one end spliced with a soft eye splice. He ran the piece through his hands, stopped, held it out to Gently. A strand of one of the twists was damaged. A section about an inch long was missing.

'From French's launch?' Gently said.

'The bow painter,' Parfitt said. 'They've been refitting all their boats with this stuff, it was the colour that made me notice.' He looked about the rond. He shivered. 'You think this would be the place?' he said.

Gently looked at the rond too. It was part dead grass, part grass in tufts. The ground under the grass was baked hard so that looking closely one saw cracks. Behind the rond and the path was the strip of meadow, across the river another stretch of bare rond. The rond across the river was grown rank with reeds but an old blue-painted houseboat was moored to it. Gently said:

'Who lives on the houseboat?'

'There's nobody on it,' Parfitt said. 'It's empty, locked up. I inquired, I couldn't learn anything about it.'

'See what you can do,' Gently said. He took a few steps about the rond. The rond was oven-hot in the sun, the dead grass wiry, unimpressible. The upturned boat which was left there to rot had nettles round it, like the *Kiama*. Her paintless straiks were whitish-grey. An angler had left some groundbait on her.

'We've got an audience,' Parfitt muttered.

He was looking towards the Spelton sheds. The two brothers and the sister were watching the policemen. They were staring at the rope which Parfitt held.

CHAPTER FIVE

THUS: SUPERINTENDENT GENTLY had lunch alone at the Country Club, while Inspector Parfitt and Detective Constable Joyce ate sandwiches and continued to prosecute their inquiries. Superintendent Gently had pineapple juice followed by ham salad in which the lettuce was cos lettuce followed by a rum baba followed by strong sweet black coffee accompanied by a small cigar or whiff. He said very little to the waitress who in turn said very little to him. He looked out of the windows at the bridge road quays and traffic and people passing over the bridge. He also looked out of the windows at the cinder path of which the first twenty yards were visible and at various times he saw William Archer crossing the bridge John French visiting the café and the humpty man identified to him as Sid Lidney passing to and fro on the cinder path. The times elapsed in these passages were William Archer's absence over the bridge one hour John French's visit to the café thirty-five minutes and between the humpty man's going and coming one hour fifty-seven minutes. Gently continued at his table until the humpty man's return. Each time he watched the humpty man closely from his appearance to his disappearance. The humpty man walked with his head down and with a slight roll of his shoulders and giving a slight snatch with his shoulders occasioned perhaps by his short legs. He looked at nobody and spoke to nobody. He wore a cap dragged forward on his head. After he had passed out of sight for the second time Gently sat still for some minutes. Then he rose.

Thus: Superintendent Gently spent a very warm afternoon assisting Inspector Parfitt and Detective Constable Joyce in the prosecution of their inquiries, and learned a great deal about waterside bungalows and the people who hired them and their habits. He found no witness who had seen Harry French on the night of Tuesday August 4th nor any witness who had seen his launch or had seen or heard any disturbance. Neither, in passing, did he find a witness who had seen a late-sailing half-decker, though he talked to several who might have seen it and even to one who knew John French. He did not talk to Rhoda Lidney. She was questioned by Detective Constable Joyce. She had only to tell him that she had spent the evening quietly indoors with her husband, Sid: seeing nothing, hearing nothing, they could ask Sid, he'd tell them the same. 'Don't do anything about Lidney,' Gently said. Nothing was done about Lidney. The owner of the old blue houseboat was not identified, although witnesses declared they had seen a man aboard her. She had no licence, no licence-holder. She had much water in her bilge.

Thus: Inspector Parfitt and Detective Constable Joyce returned to Starmouth with their evidence, and Superintendent Gently ate his evening meal at the Country Club. While he ate lights suddenly sparkled on the canopy of the Cakewalk across the bridge, machinery rumbled beneath the canopy and 'Valencia' crashed newborn into the warm still evening. Craft were moored touching and overlapping on the quays and the ronds opposite, tomorrow being handover day with handover time at ten a.m. Crews from these boats wandered over the bridge shouldered about the fairground stood in aimless groups filled the bars and garden of the Bridge Inn sat in the café sought tables in the Country Club. As yet they still wore their boat clothes. They were brown and golden from a fine week. They spoke in Midland accents for the most part also northern accents and some cockney. They moved slowly lingeringly lazily riverlike having time to watch talk get a little drunk on the last night. Some had met Harry French when they set sail some hadn't even heard he was dead. Their tide was ebbing, tomorrow a new tide would run, 'Valencia' changing to 'Harvest Moon' changing to 'Donna Clara' changing to 'Ramona'. All this Gently saw while he was eating his evening meal.

Thus: he also saw the humpty man and John French coming out of the café the humpty man looking about him with puckered eyes John French with shoulders hunched his hands in his pockets the humpty man talking John French listening the humpty man motioning with his head several times towards the cinder path John French hanging back the humpty man making gestures talking John French shrugging the humpty man nodding the humpty man turning and going up the cinder path John French turning and going slowly over towards the yard.

Thus: Gently rose from his table and followed John French.

John French continued walking very slowly across the yard and came at last to a side mooring dyke in which several workboats were moored. He stood by the dyke, looked at the boats, kicked some gravel into the dyke, looked at his father's launch, which was also moored there, scuffed at the gravel, stood. Then after a few minutes during which time his hands had remained in his pockets he removed his hands from his pockets, stooped, untied the outermost workboat and stepped aboard it. He pulled over the engine and the engine started. He steered the boat into the main dyke and towards the river. On reaching the river he pointed the boat downstream and opened the throttle a little further. He didn't look backwards towards the bridge but forward towards some upcoming craft and so he didn't see the launch *White Heron* leaving the Country Club dyke near the bridge. He sat by the tiller of the workboat with one hand returned to his pocket. His head was inclined forward. He steered precisely and without attention.

The workboat went through the bungalows and by a small dilapidated yard and by a brick pumpmill tower without sails or cap but with a huge toothed wheel slanted out of the top of it and by the speed-limit signs

and by a public staithe dyke to the left and by a brick
and thatch cottage below the rond wall which cottage
was advertising fresh eggs and so to half a mile of reed
ronds behind which black-and-white cattle grazed on
grazing marsh and a dyke proceeding to the right
towards trees higher ground and a square flint church-
tower. John French turned the workboat into this dyke.
The dyke twisted like a country lane. It passed the dyke
and quays of a yard where were moored a fleet of
rosewood-coloured yachts. It passed lawns entered alder
carrs entered a small broad with a public quay resumed
at the far end of the broad under tall weeping willow
trees where a board said Private. Beyond this board it
was hemmed with weeping willow trees till it ended at
a quay at the foot of a lawn and above the lawn a
yellowbrick house and above the house copper beeches.
Here John French moored the workboat. He stepped
ashore, went straight up the lawn. The lawn was
bounded by rhododendrons and azaleas and fuschias and
begonia beds. The front of the house which faced the
lawn had twin bows with tall sash windows and between
the bows french windows and in all the windows slatted
blinds. John French didn't look at these. He crossed a
gravel path and turned right. He passed through a
garden door into a tiled yard and through a kitchen door
into a large kitchen. A woman was ironing in the
kitchen. The kitchen smelled of heated linen. The
woman was elderly and stout and wore a blue scarf on
her head and had on plaid slippers. She tilted the iron
when John French came in, looked at John French. He
looked at her. The woman said:

94

'So you're back Mr John. I didn't know whether to have a meal ready for you.'

'I'd have rung if I'd wanted one,' John French said. 'Have they been on the phone again?'

'Yes, they have,' the woman said. 'Your uncle's been on the phone twice. Being very obstinate you are, he says, you ought to let one of them stay here till it's all over.'

'He can go to hell,' John French said.

'Well I think he's right,' the woman said.

'He's not setting foot in here,' John French said. 'None of them are. They can all go to hell. They snubbed us enough when my father was alive, now I'm doing the snubbing. They can go to hell. Who else rang up?'

'Mr Laskey. He'd like to have an appointment, you're to ring back,' the woman said.

'Damned old crow,' John French said. 'He'll make a packet out of it if nobody else does. Anyone else.'

'No,' the woman said.

'Have the police been back here?'

'No,' the woman said.

'Don't look at me in that way,' John French said. 'For heaven's sake, Beattie, cheer yourself up.'

The woman sniffed, dropped her eyes to the ironing board. 'I don't know, Mr John,' she said, 'I keep carrying on, I tell myself I'll stand by you. But I don't know what I'm going to do.'

'Beattie,' John French said.

'It's been such a shock, such a shock,' the woman said. 'And the way you carry on. It isn't natural Mr John.

Seems like everything's gone to pieces, I just don't dare to think about it.'

'You've been up to the village,' John French said. The woman nodded, sniffing.

'I know,' John French said. 'I know what they've been saying to you. You were all right this morning, Beattie, you could look me in the eyes then.'

'Mr John,' the woman said.

'Then if that's the way you want it,' John French said. 'I'm not crawling to anyone Beattie, you can damn well believe what you want to believe. I don't care, I know what I know. If you want to sling your hook you can sling it. Go on, get out. Just leave me here. Perhaps you think you aren't safe, I'll do something to you.'

'Oh Mr John,' the woman said.

'I thought I could trust you,' John French said. 'I thought you were someone who knew me, Beattie. I thought I could trust you if nobody else.'

'It's been such a shock,' the woman sobbed.

'So what's it been like to me?' John French said. 'It's me who the police are trying to catch out, it was my old man who was hit over the head.'

The woman wept.

'And now you,' John French said. 'The only one I had to depend on. And you've turned against me with the rest, you're ready to leave me to face it alone.'

'There's your mother's people,' the woman sobbed.

'I've told you I won't have them here,' John French said. 'They'd love to come here pushing me around, but nobody's going to push me around any more. Just get out if that's what you want. I'd sooner you did. Then I'll know where I stand.'

His face was working. The woman sobbed. The smell of heated linen filled the kitchen. John French was trembling and clenching his hands in his pockets. From the tilted iron came simmering noises.

'Beattie,' John French said. 'I didn't Beattie. I didn't. I didn't.'

The woman went on sobbing.

'I didn't. I didn't.' John French said, 'Beattie. Don't you believe me?'

'Oh Mr John,' the woman said.

'It's just . . . damnable,' John French said. 'But I didn't, Beattie. That's the truth. Remember it Beattie. It wasn't me.'

He turned quickly, went out of the kitchen, turned down a hallway, entered the drawing room. This was the room between the bows and had the french windows looking down the lawn. It smelled of dust and faded flowers and was warm and airless from being closed up. Also it smelled of stale cigar smoke and an opened box of Coronas lay on a low coffee table. A big room. Contemporary furniture. Ash-grey timber with cream contrast. At one end the low flattened ebony case of the late Mrs French's grand piano. John French closed the door behind him and turned the key in the lock of the door. He crossed to the other side of the room where on the wall hung an Edmund Seago oil painting. He pulled on the frame of the painting. The painting swung on hinges. Behind the painting was apparently a baize backing-sheet but this was mounted on wood and also swung on hinges. John French pulled this open too. Behind it was a large Chubb wall safe with a combination lock. John French began to operate the combination lock, bending close to the safe, pausing after each dialling. He tried the handle. The handle wouldn't turn. He wiped his face, dialled again. This time the handle turned smoothly and the heavy safe-door moved outwards. He searched in the safe. It was stuffed with paper, documents, letters, pass-books, envelopes. Harry French's marriage certificate, two out-of-date passports, a mass of title-deeds secured with tape, a copy of Mrs French's will. At last, from a drawer, a long thick envelope sealed with wax and Harry French's seal. John French tore it open. It contained five-pound notes. They were in bundles of fifty and there were six bundles. John French laid the envelope on the floor while he repacked the safe and closed it, then he tried to cram the envelope into his inside jacket pocket, failed, stuck it underneath his arm beneath the jacket. He crossed to the door, unlocked it, went down the hallway into the kitchen. Eleven minutes had elapsed. The woman had gone back to her ironing.

'Beattie,' John French said.

The woman raised her head, looked at him.

'I've to go out again, Beattie,' John French said. 'I'll try not to be late, it's some business I've got to see to.'

'Very well Mr John,' the woman said.

'Beattie,' John French said. 'It's all right, isn't it?'

'I'll be here when you come back if that's what you mean,' the woman said.

John French nodded. 'Thanks Beattie,' he said,

'thanks.' The woman kept on ironing. John French went out of the kitchen.

He crossed the tiled yard to the garden door, holding the envelope tightly, went through the garden door, collided with somebody outside it. The envelope fell. John French grabbed after it. Another hand was there first. John French made a second grab for it. Still he didn't have the envelope.

Superintendent Gently had the envelope and John French attempted no third grab. He stood staring at the Superintendent, mouth thinned, lids expanded. The Superintendent glanced at the envelope, at the seal, at the contents; at John French. He tapped the envelope on the palm of his hand.

'Your property?' he said.

'Just give it back to me,' John French said.

'But it is your property?' Gently said.

'You damn well know it's my property,' John French said.

'I know you took it from your father's safe,' Gently said, 'and that you needed two shots at the combination. And that the seal bears your father's monogram. And that you were concealing your possession of it. What would that suggest to you?'

'Never mind about that,' John French said. 'You give it back to me or there'll be trouble. I'm not going to argue. Give it back.'

'Perhaps your father was keeping it safe for you,' Gently said. 'In that case you're entitled to do what you like with it.'

'So give it back to me,' John French said. 'I told you it was mine. He was just keeping it safe.'

'Then,' Gently said, 'how did you come by it? It's a lot of cash for a young student to have around.'

John French stared very hard at Gently, at the envelope. His cheek was twitching.

'Look,' he said, 'what the hell does it matter whether it was my father's money or mine. It's all the same now, he's dead, there's no difference, it comes to me. They told me I could draw what I needed. It's got damn all to do with you at all.'

'Not if it's your money,' Gently said.

'It is my money,' John French said.

'But if it's your father's,' Gently said, 'It has to do with me, you're committing an offence. The money is part of his estate, it doesn't become yours till you get probate. So if you can't show your title to it you'd better put it back in the safe.'

'But I need it,' John French said. 'My lawyer said I could draw some money.'

'From the business earnings,' Gently said, 'not from the estate. And why do you need fifteen hundred pounds?'

John French said nothing, bit his lips together. He looked sideways into the tiled yard. Like a pulse of blood, very far away, one heard the thumping of the Cakewalk. At last he said:

'All right, I didn't know. I thought it was all right to use the money. If it isn't I'll put it back. It was only a loan, anyway, till I can touch my own money. I'm not a pauper. I've got the money mother left me. I'm only waiting for the rotten lawyers to clear it.'

'That would be sensible,' Gently said. 'When is your mother's legacy due?'

'I should have it now,' John French said. 'When I came of age. It was due on Tuesday.'

'You were twenty-one on Tuesday,' Gently said.

'All right, I can't help it,' John French said. 'I didn't arrange when I was going to have my birthday. Do you think I'm happy about it or something?'

'It didn't seem to be panning out like a birthday,' Gently said, 'and a twenty-first birthday at that. Beginning with a quarrel with your father and ending with you going off on your own. And then some impediment about your legacy.'

'Who says there's an impediment?' John French said.

'You did,' Gently said. 'But I can talk to your lawyers.'

John French didn't say anything.

'Not much like a birthday,' Gently said.

'Can't you ever stop prying?' John French said. 'Even following me about now, watching me through windows.'

'Perhaps you needed that money on Tuesday,' Gently said. 'Perhaps you discovered your father was interfering. But what would you need a large sum of money for? What would you need it for tonight?'

'Look,' John French said, 'just stop it. I won't be pushed around like this. I'm not even safe from it in my own home, you've no right to come here like this. You just get out.'

'I'd say that Sid asked for it,' Gently said.

'Nobody gave you permission to come here,' John French said.

'And that you couldn't say no to him,' Gently said.

'Give it to me, give it to me,' John French said. 'I'll ring my lawyer. Give it to me. Clear off.'

Gently didn't give it to him. John French didn't move towards a phone. They stood facing each other, staring. John French's mouth was very small. It was getting dusk but not cooler. The beeches, the willows below were heavily dark. Moths bobbed in the flowerbeds, bats pipped, in the beeches were wood pigeons. John French's eyes were glittering. Suddenly the kitchen door closed.

'Do you know where your father was killed?' Gently said.

John French didn't say anything.

'He was killed on that patch of rond above the bridge,' Gently said. 'Between the bungalows and Speltons' sheds. He'd driven the launch to that rond. He went to visit someone and then returned. And then he was killed. As he untied the launch. But who could it have been he went there to visit?'

John French didn't say anything.

'It could have been the Speltons,' Gently said.

John French said huskily: 'They've been working late.'

'Yes,' Gently said. 'I see you know that.'

'And why the hell shouldn't I know that?' John French said. 'They're friends of mine aren't they. I know what they're doing.'

'You might also have seen a light in the sheds,' Gently said, 'if you were passing there late. You might have seen quite a lot. But why should your father visit the Speltons?'

'Why am I supposed to know?' John French said.

'So late,' Gently said, 'not mooring at their quay. Going up without lights. Trying not to be seen.'

'I tell you I don't know,' John French said.

'Perhaps he was going somewhere else,' Gently said.

'All right then he was,' John French said.

'Where?' Gently said. 'And for what purpose?'

'I don't know, I don't know,' John French said.

'Surely,' Gently said, 'it must have been to Sid's place. All the other bungalows near the rond are hire bungalows. We've found nobody in the hire bungalows with any connection with your father. You say you don't know why he should visit the Speltons. It only leaves Sid.'

'Why are you asking me about it,' John French said. 'I just don't know, I keep telling you, I don't know.'

'But of course, you were at Sid's place,' Gently said. 'What other reason did your father have for going there so secretly?'

John French breathed hard. 'I was out sailing,' he said. 'I wasn't anywhere near Sid's place except coming down the river going past it.'

'Yes, you were there,' Gently said. 'Otherwise it doesn't fit. And now he's demanding a large sum of money and you are ready to pay it to him.'

'No,' John French said, 'no.'

'Then where was this money going?' Gently said.

'I'm putting it back aren't I?' John French said.

'Yes,' Gently said, 'but where was it going?'

John French didn't say anything. His nostrils were expanded by his heavy breathing. His eyes were below

103

Gently's now. The eyes were big and dark in the dim light. The throb of the Cakewalk and the tapping of moths underlined the sound of John French's breathing. The warm air smelled of grass and mint and peat and river and night-scented stock.

'How long had you been intimate with Rhoda Lidney?' Gently said.

John French licked his lips, said: 'It's a lie, it's all a lie.'

'Weren't you spending money on her?' Gently said, 'weren't they after you for money? Threatening to tell your father perhaps. Using all the tricks of the trade.'

'No,' John French said, 'lies.'

'But they wanted money from you,' Gently said. 'They knew you were coming into some money, they had a plan for getting hold of it. And somehow your father got wind of this. That was how it was, wasn't it? And the money wasn't there on your birthday, your father had done some jiggerypokery.'

'Lies, lies,' John French said.

'So you had a row about it,' Gently said.

'There wasn't any row,' John French said.

'How loyal is your housekeeper?' Gently said.

John French didn't say anything.

'You had a row about it,' Gently said. 'And you had to tell Sid that you didn't have his money for him and in the evening you went down to his bungalow. And your father came looking for you at the bungalow and he found out everything. And he died.'

'No,' John French said, 'not like that.'

'Perhaps you can give me some details,' Gently said.

'I,' John French said, 'I was out sailing. It's all lies, all lies.'

'You weren't out sailing,' Gently said. 'We've spoken to witnesses who must have seen you. They didn't see you, you weren't sailing. You were at the bungalow and nowhere else.'

'You're calling me a liar,' John French said.

'I may have to call you something worse,' Gently said.

'It's you who's the liar,' John French said. 'You're lying, lying, lying, lying.'

'This isn't doing you any good,' Gently said. 'Can't you see that only the truth will help you? You're standing one step away from the dock. Tomorrow, the next day, we'll have you in it. Tell me the truth.'

'But I'm telling it,' John French said. 'I've told it all along and you won't believe me. I didn't kill my father, I didn't, I didn't, that's the truth, I didn't kill my father.'

'Then you know who did,' Gently said.

'No I don't know who did,' John French said. 'I wasn't there, I didn't see it. I don't know who did it. I just don't know.'

'But who could have done it?' Gently said.

'Oh God oh God,' John French said.

'I don't think you should be paying Sid money,' Gently said. 'I think perhaps he should be paying it to you.'

John French swayed, scraped his foot in the gravel. He closed his eyes, said: 'I – just – don't – know. Not anything about it. Nothing about it. Nothing, nothing about it. Nothing.'

'Yet you were there,' Gently said.

'I was out sailing,' John French said.

'But of course, you weren't out sailing,' Gently said.

105

'I was out sailing,' John French said.

'Now we've proved you weren't out sailing,' Gently said.

'I,' John French said, 'was out sailing. In a half-decker. Up to Hickstead. Out sailing. Where I went.'

'But you're a liar,' Gently said.

John French swayed, didn't say anything.

'Tell me the truth,' Gently said.

John French said: 'Out sailing.'

'Let's start at the beginning,' Gently said. 'Tell me about the row with your father.'

'No there wasn't a row,' John French said. 'Haven't I told you? There wasn't a row.'

'Yes, about the legacy,' Gently said. 'What sort of game was he up to?'

'Nothing,' John French said. 'Nothing. Nothing, nothing.'

'But that's a lie,' Gently said.

'It's all lies,' John French said.

'Tell me the truth,' Gently said.

'Nothing,' John French said. 'Nothing.'

He kept repeating 'Nothing', swaying a little, his eyes shut. There was a movement in the tiled yard. The woman called Beattie appeared at the doorway. She looked at Gently. Her eyes moved quickly, sank again after meeting his. She fidgeted. Her age was about sixty, she had a plump face that was sagging.

'Yes,' Gently said.

'It's right,' she said. 'There wasn't any row between Mr John and his father.'

'I see,' Gently said. 'Are you the housekeeper?'

106

'Beattie Playford,' the woman said.

John French opened his eyes.

'I got the breakfast,' the woman said. 'They were pleasant enough together. Mr John had a gold watch from his father.'

'How interesting,' Gently said.

'Yes,' the woman said, 'a gold watch, one of them self-winders, you know. Got engraving on the back. He'll show it to you if you ask him. Then they was talking, I don't know, about all the boats being out for August. I don't listen to what they say. But they weren't having a row.'

'Very interesting,' Gently said. 'What colour tie was Mr French wearing?'

'It, it was blue,' the woman said. 'Yes, that's it, a blue tie.'

John French said: 'No. No tie.'

'Yes, that's right,' the woman said. 'No tie, I'm forgetting, that must have been some other day.'

'Perhaps you're forgetting about the row,' Gently said.

'No,' the woman said, 'I'm not forgetting.'

'They did have rows, didn't they?' Gently said.

The woman kept her head down, didn't say anything.

John French said: 'If you want to see the watch—'

Gently shook his head. 'I'll believe the watch,' he said.

'I'll fetch it, show it to you,' John French said. 'Then you won't be able to say it's a lie.'

Gently stood silent for several moments. He tapped the envelope on his knuckles. Then he shrugged, held it out to John French. 'Here,' he said, 'take the money.'

John French looked at him.

'Take the money,' Gently said.

John French put out his hand. His hand was shaking. Gently put the envelope in it. John French took the envelope.

'I wouldn't bother to see Sid again tonight,' Gently said. 'Sid'll be otherwise engaged. And don't pay Sid any money. There's nothing useful it can buy.'

John French said quickly: 'You, you've got it wrong.'

'How wrong?' Gently said.

John French shook his head, was silent. After a moment Gently turned and went down the lawn.

CHAPTER SIX

T HUS: SUPERINTENDENT GENTLY drove back to Haynor in the launch *White Heron* when it was nearly
dark on the evening of Friday August 7th. The water
was pallid between heavy-shadowed banks and smoking
with fine white mist and the mist hovered in level strata
in motionless continents and islands. Lamps were lit in
the moored craft which were all large because of the
darkness and the light of the lamps was orange-yellow
and the boats looked hollow and big inside. Below each
lamp a serpent wriggled in the water. About the serpents
the water was heavy and glasslike. The flaps of awnings
were tied back showing dim outer caves leading to lit
inner caves in which mahogany glowed reddishly. In the
inner caves people sat eating smoking talking laughing.
Occasionally an outer cave was lit and there people were
cooking or washing dishes. The mooring ropes of the
boats disappeared into the blackness of the rond and
the marshes and the alder carrs and the reedbeds and the
silence. Past these *White Heron* slid into the shanty street
of the bungalows with Reuben's lights prickling bluely

beyond the stretched silhouette of roofs with Reuben's Cakewalk hammering the sky and traffic mounting the black bridge and the square flat-roofed building of French's yard bulking faintly above these. Nothing passed her on the way. The traffic tide was at slack water. Single and double at the quays the lit yachts burned the water. Reuben's lights gashed the water and it was oily where the lights gashed it. People walked along the ronds. People laughed, called to each other. At the Country Club mooring a man was standing and passing car lights showed the man to be Archer. Archer was watching *White Heron*. *White Heron* came slowly in to the Club mooring. Archer didn't move away. Gently stepped ashore, moored.

Archer said: 'You're breaking rules, should've had lights coming up here.'

'I'm always breaking rules,' Gently said. 'What would it have cost me, breaking that one?'

'Christ knows,' Archer said. 'There's never anyone around to book you for it. The police pack up about teatime. Anything goes on the Broads.'

'Are you working this late?' Gently said.

Archer shook his head very slowly. 'Wife's a nagger,' he said. 'She was on a nagging jag tonight. I didn't strangle her, perhaps I ought to. Do you think I ought to strangle her? But no, I'm forgetting, that's one of the rules you wouldn't break. Anyway I didn't strangle her. I was strong. I came out to booze. Maybe tomorrow I'll strangle her. I don't know. Stick around.'

'Did you want to talk to me?' Gently said.

'Hell no, not especially,' Archer said. 'I see you

haven't brought back young French in handcuffs, I thought you would when you followed him off.'

'Why did you think that?' Gently said.

'I'm a philosopher,' Archer said. 'I get like that on Friday nights. No particular reason I know of. All the week I'm as miserable as sin and the more bottles the more I'm miserable. Maybe it takes a week to tank me up, I wouldn't know. It's a theory.'

'You're not drunk,' Gently said.

'Listen to the policeman,' Archer said. 'Maybe they'll cop me when I drive home and then I'll call you as evidence, that'll be a laugh.'

'You've been watching me,' Gently said.

'Who guards the guardians,' Archer said. 'Don't you like being watched, Mr Policeman?'

Gently didn't say anything.

'On Friday nights,' Archer said. 'Haynor belongs to me, Fridays. All the damage is done then, nobody bashes a boat on Fridays. Nobody bashes Harry French on Fridays. I don't strangle my wife on Fridays. You don't arrest young French on Fridays. What do you say I buy you a drink?'

'Why were you watching me?' Gently said.

'It's a habit,' Archer said. 'I can't break it.'

'Why are you pretending to be drunk?' Gently said.

'It's cheaper,' Archer said, 'a darn sight cheaper. Do you know what they charge for Scotch these days, not the cheap stuff, genuine Scotch? It's wicked, the government are killing the business. It costs me a fiver a day to keep sozzled. And now they've mucked about with methylated spirits so it makes your eyes pop out of

111

your head, it's getting grim, that's a fact. You need to be a five-figure man.'

'You're not a five-figure man,' Gently said.

'I rob the till,' Archer said.

'You know more than you've told me,' Gently said.

'Well I've only known you five minutes,' Archer said.

'Why should John French pay Lidney money?' Gently said.

Archer hiccupped. 'That's naughty,' he said.

'Why have you promoted Lidney?' Gently said.

'The system,' Archer said. 'Promotion. The system.'

'Did John French tell you to promote Lidney?'

'No,' Archer said, 'my goodness of heart. Can't keep a good man down for ever. Got to promote him. That's the system.'

'Did you promote someone else to make room for him?'

'New creation,' Archer said. 'In charge of boat's furniture.'

'Straight after Harry French was murdered,' Gently said. 'Lidney gets promoted. Just like that.'

Archer waved his hand uncertainly. 'Don't confuse me,' he said. 'For a policeman I like you, I like you a lot. But don't confuse me. Keep it simple. You want a drink?'

'Why did you promote him?'

'Here we go,' Archer said. 'On and on and on and on. Just like my wife. Just like Gladys. You want a drink boy, that's what. You want to forget all this ballsing. It isn't doing you any good. What sort of life is it, I ask you.'

'I'll tell you why you promoted him,' Gently said. 'It's

because Lidney is a key witness. And that's why John French is going to pay him money. Lidney has got you by the short hairs.'

Archer swerved, stuck his foot out, rocked himself steady. His long face and pendulous nose silhouetted a moment against Reuben's lights.

'I don't know,' he said. 'It beats me, why I like you. You're a rotten bastard, but I like you. Harry was a rotten bastard. I liked him. I'm a pushover for rotten bastards. My wife's another, I like her. Rotten bastards. I reckon they fascinate me. If I was weak I'd be a rotten bastard. I can't help myself that way. I attract them. Somehow.'

'We could sober you up in a cell,' Gently said.

'Waste of time,' Archer said. 'Drunk or sober I'm always the same. I'm me. You can't alter it.'

'You're at Lidney's beck and call,' Gently said. 'Do you want that situation to last? Do you want to go on getting drunk so you can forget it? The degradation, you like that?'

'Go on,' Archer said. 'I like it. Rotten bastards are meat and drink to me. Not meat, just drink, I'm a sort of vegetarian.'

'You're a fool,' Gently said. 'Nobody can cover up a murder. There'll be a lot of you pulled in as accessories if you keep on lying and covering up.'

'Should I care?' Archer said. 'Pull them all in boy. Fill the prisons top to bottom, make a clean sweep all round. That's life, filling the prisons. You keep building them and filling them. The commies fill them with one sort, the cappies fill them with another. What's the difference? Have a drink. You're out in the country here boy.'

'Yes,' Gently said, 'out in the country.'

'Commies and cappies,' Archer said. 'I'm an anarchist myself but I never remember to be political.'

Gently didn't say anything. People came across the bridge. The thumping rhythm of the Cakewalk was backed by the rumble of a coach, a truck. The river was stealing towards the Sounds, showed upward-moving where light fell on it. Somebody was falling around, shouting, in a moored dinghy. More people came across the bridge.

'Friday night,' Archer said. 'Haynor belongs to me, Fridays. Only a common old working man with a couple of dozen drinks inside me. Another August Bank Holiday. So Harry French has to die. Nothing special. I'm a liar if I say it's anything special. Go back to London and forget about it. We shan't cheek the local copper.'

'When did you last see the Speltons?' Gently said.

'Just forget about it boy,' Archer said.

'I want an answer,' Gently said.

'Disappointment unlimited,' Archer said.

Gently said: 'I don't know if you realize it, but none of you have an alibi worth tuppence. You haven't. The Speltons haven't. The Lidneys haven't. John French hasn't. None of you have got alibis. All of you were here. All of you gain something from Harry French's death. All of you are lying or being obstructive. Every one of you stands close to being arrested. You may be arrested in a bunch. That's the situation, Mr Archer. You'd better sober up and think about it.'

'You have to say it,' Archer said. 'That's your job. You have to say it. But you're a decent bastard too, I'm an expert on bastards. Look, we're people. I'm one. You aren't going to say I'm not one. I'm a comic bastard. My wife nags me. I hit the bottle. You can laugh at me. We're all like that, we're people. We don't go around killing each other. Nobody can remember a murder here. It isn't like London, isn't like Starmouth. Look, I was standing here this morning, see, after you'd bollicked me in the office, and there was a cruiser moored over the other side with a couple of blokes on board it. They'd finished breakfast, were starting off. They were turning up to go through the bridge. One of the blokes was at the wheel, the other was tidying the mooring rope forrard. And the one forrard turned to come aft and he turned outwards instead of inwards and he just walked over the side and disappeared and the bloke at the wheel didn't see it. They never do see it when it happens. It's always casual, like that. There's some bloody thing about motor-cruisers that drowns people even people who can swim. So we saw it and pulled him out and he was shaking like an aspen. But we needn't have seen it, needn't have pulled him out, he was just bloody lucky. That's the way they die round here. Who'd have been to blame for drowning him? We built that cruiser. Hookers let it. You going to arrest us in a bunch? We murder several like that in the season, it's one of the conditions of the business. You won't see it mentioned in Hookers' catalogue but you'll see it mentioned in the coroner's records.'

'So,' Gently said.

'So,' Archer said. 'It was like that, just like that.

Maybe someone's to blame, I wouldn't know, but not the sort of blame you should put them away for. More like an accident, that's how. Like somebody walking off a cruiser. It's a bad business, but it isn't murder. You're to blame for the murder part. Just get drunk. Forget about it. You're not doing good, you're doing harm. Let it heal. Stop using the knife. You're dealing with people. The law's an ass.'

'Supposing you're murdered next?' Gently said.

'I'm wasting my time,' Archer said. 'Never mind, Friday night. You go on playing detectives boy.'

'I'm not playing,' Gently said.

'Don't confuse me,' Archer said. 'You're playing detectives. You play a good game boy. Friday night. Have your fun.'

He swerved again, checked himself, reached into the pocket of his jacket. He brought out a quarter flask of whisky, uncapped it, put the bottle in his mouth and tilted it. His throat worked. The lights of a bus showed his eyes expanded, looking at Gently. The smell of the whisky came to Gently. Archer finished drinking and recapped the bottle.

'Nothing special,' he said. 'You're out in the country, nothing special. Why do you kick it around so much?'

Gently nodded. 'Yes,' he said.

Thus: Superintendent Gently crossed the road near the bridge while William Archer remained standing at the mooring and Reuben's Cakewalk was playing 'Dark Eyes': and Superintendent Gently took the cinder path between Speltons' sheds and the Country Club and noticed in passing that there was a light in the sheds but that the Spelton house opposite them was unlit. He continued along the cinder path and stopped at the gate of the seventh bungalow. He went through the gate to the back door of the bungalow and rapped on the door with the knocker. A door creaked in the bungalow. Shuffling steps approached the outer door. A bolt was shot and the door opened and a woman stood there at first smilingly. She wore a blue worsted dressing gown and fur-trimmed slippers and the dressing gown was worn carelessly and there was nothing under the dressing gown; she wasn't young she had a matronly figure but it was strong and aggressive, she had gold-blonde hair, blue eyes, a large thin-lipped mouth with spidery lines coming from it. She smelled of cloves perhaps carnation. After the smile her eyes were hard. She stood still without adjusting her dressing gown. She looked at Gently he looked at her. She said:

'What's the lark now?'

'Superintendent Gently,' Gently said. 'Mrs Lidney.'

'Who did you think,' she said. 'Marilyn Monroe's kicked the bucket.'

'Is your husband in?' Gently said.

'What do you want him for?' Mrs Lidney said.

'I've some questions to ask him,' Gently said. 'You too. About Tuesday night.'

'Well Sid isn't in,' Mrs Lidney said. 'So your questions had better wait till the morning hadn't they.'

'Where is Sid?' Gently said.

'Ask me another,' Mrs Lidney said. 'Gone out for a drink maybe.'

She had a masculine voice which was gritty. She was taller than average. Her big breasts pushed the dressing gown apart and the nipples were spreading and livid and warted. The dressing gown was held together with a tie but below the tie her thighs showed. The thighs were large and blanched and veined and the knees smallish and the calves full.

'You wanna come in?' Mrs. Lidney said.

'Yes,' Gently said, 'I'd like to come in.'

'Taking a risk aren't you?' Mrs Lidney said. 'I thought you always went after the women in pairs.'

'I can talk to you out here,' Gently said. 'It isn't private but it'll do.'

'Do you think I'm going to eat you?' Mrs Lidney said. 'I don't give a frig. You can come in.'

She moved away from the door. Gently went in. She closed the door. They stood in a hallway running through the bungalow to a door with coloured glass panes in the front of the bungalow. The hallway was papered with rust flower-pattern paper and the paper was not new. The hallway was lit by a single bulb and had two doors leading off it on each side. By the wall near the door with the coloured glass panes stood an iron doorstop which was shaped like an anchor.

'Up there on the left,' Mrs Lidney said.

Gently went up the hallway, she came behind him. He stopped. He looked at the doorstop. The clove smell of the woman was close beside him.

'Your doorstop is bent,' Gently said.

'Damn near everything's bent here,' Mrs Lidney said.

'Looks as though it might have been thrown at something,' Gently said.

'Well it wouldn't have been the first time,' Mrs Lidney said.

Gently stooped, picked up the doorstop. It weighed about seven pounds. The anchor it represented was a fisherman's anchor but with the stock on the same plane as the arms. The crown was nested in a display of seashells which formed the heavy base of the stop and a twisted cable descended from the ring to form a letter S about the shank. The stock had balls at each end. The extremity of each ball was flattened. The left-hand arm of the stock was bent and the flat surface of its ball showed a silvery graze. There were smaller grazes on other parts of the stop which was painted black and showed grazes clearly.

'So what was it thrown at?' Gently said.

'How the hell should I know,' Mrs Lidney said. 'Maybe the cat from next door, it's a ginger tom, Sid can't stick it.'

'Is Sid usually so violent?' Gently said.

'Who says he's violent?' Mrs Lidney said. 'If a dirty thieving cat came poohing in your yard wouldn't you chuck something at it, wouldn't you?'

'I didn't know you had resident neighbours,' Gently said.

'All right we haven't then,' Mrs Lidney said. 'I don't know where the bloody cat comes from, and another thing hangs to it. I don't care.'

Gently said nothing. He looked along the hallway. The hallway was laid with buff boat's lino. The lino was old and darkened and scuffed and had dust and fluff lying on it. Near one of the further doors the lino was bruised with a heavy bruise and a lighter bruise and the heavy bruise was circular and fractured the surface to show fresh raw cork. Gently took the doorstop to the bruising. He laid a flattened ball in the heavy bruise. The flattened ball fitted. In the bruise was light dust and a piece of trapped fluff. All about the bruising and higher up the hallway were deep scratches and fresh scuff-marks and on the wallpaper near the scuff-marks were five kick-marks showing black. The woman hadn't moved from the hallway. She stood still. She watched Gently.

'Quite a cat,' Gently said.

'Oh to hell with cats,' Mrs Lidney said.

Gently came back to her. 'Who was fighting?' he said. 'Who threw this doorstop? Who was he throwing it at?'

'Don't know what you mean,' Mrs Lidney said. 'What fighting? There hasn't been no fighting. It's a lot of balls about the fighting. Nobody's done any fighting here.'

'Yes,' Gently said, 'they were doing some fighting. On Tuesday night they were doing some fighting. Harry French's body has got marks on it. There's a graze on the shoulder where he was hit with something heavy. The graze was inflicted shortly before his death. It was inflicted by something like this doorstop. And there's a hole in Harry French's skull. It was inflicted by something like one of these balls. And Harry French came through the bridge on Tuesday and he moored on the rond a hundred yards below here.'

'So what, so what,' Mrs Lidney said.

'So he came here,' Gently said, 'and there was a fight with your husband.'

'Cross my heart it's a bloody lie,' Mrs Lidney said. 'He never came here at all nor didn't nobody that night.'

'Then who was fighting?' Gently said. 'Who threw this doorstop? Who was he throwing it at?'

The woman stared at him. Her lids were widened. Her spidery mouth-lines were drawn deep. Along with the smell of cloves that came from her was the smell of perspiration. Her body was slightly thrown back from her hips and her elbows were bent and her fingers crooked.

'All right you prying sod,' she said. 'Then I did have a fight with my old man. Now you know perhaps you're happy. And I did throw the bloody stopper at him. Pity I didn't hit him too. He'd have laughed on the other side of his face. And what the hell's it got to do with you or Harry French or any other bugger?'

'Do you have a telephone?' Gently said.

'No I don't have a telephone,' Mrs Lidney said. 'I don't have a coffee-shop with a flush either, anything else you want to know?'

Gently set down the doorstop, took out a notebook. He drew a sketch-plan of the hallway of the bungalow. On the sketch-plan he marked the bruises and indicated the areas of the scratches and scuff-marks and kick-marks. The woman watched him with big eyes. Gently added notes to the sketch-plan. The woman's breathing which had been fast began to subside while Gently was writing. Gently put the notebook away, picked up the doorstop, hefted it.

'You don't bloody well believe me do you?' Mrs Lidney said. 'If I swore it on a Bible you wouldn't believe what I told you. I can't help it, that's your lookout. You're going to shift the blame on to someone. Perhaps you think we've got a bad name, you can shift it on to us easy.'

'How long has John French been visiting you?' Gently said.

'Didn't know he had been visiting me,' Mrs Lidney said.

'He admits he's been here,' Gently said.

'Oh and very nice too,' Mrs Lidney said. 'So he admits he's been here does he? I'll have something to say to him about that. Dragging my name in the mud, bringing the police snooping round here. What else does he say?'

'How much did he pay you?' Gently said.

'The damn little liar,' Mrs Lidney said. 'He's never paid me anything, I've never had a penny off him.'

'Never?' Gently said.

'Never,' Mrs Lidney said. 'Cross my heart I never asked him for it. What do you think I am anyway?'

'What did his father think you were?' Gently said.

'Oh go and jump in the river,' Mrs Lidney said. 'You're all alike the last one of you. It's a different thing when you want your under. If he did come round here whose business is that, what's it got to do with you lot? It didn't do him any harm I can tell you that. He needed someone to take him in hand.'

'And his father knew?' Gently said.

'Why don't you go down to the mortuary and ask him?' Mrs Lidney said.

'And knew about the money angle,' Gently said.

'Oh Christalmighty,' Mrs Lidney said. 'It was bloody free. Can't I get it across to you. Free, for nothing, I throw it in. I like a kid to cut some off with.'

'But money came into it,' Gently said.

'Money didn't come into it,' Mrs Lidney said.

'Sid was getting money out of it,' Gently said.

'Fall under a bus,' Mrs Lidney said. 'Fall under a bus.'

'Sid was putting the screw on tonight,' Gently said.

Mrs Lidney looked at him, didn't say anything.

'Quite a big screw,' Gently said. 'What could it be, now the father is dead?'

The back-door latch lifted softly. The woman's eyes jerked towards it. Gently turned towards the door. The door opened. The humpty man entered. He stood squinting towards them, his eyes tiny, sharpened. His eyes fell on the doorstop. He closed the door slowly behind him. He said:

'Hullo Rhoda. I could hear you'd got company.'

He took some steps up the hallway, stopped, peered at Gently.

'Yes,' the humpty man said to Gently, 'I know who you are. Got a nerve haven't you, coming here talking to Rhoda at this time of night. I could report you for that mate. You could get yourself into trouble. I dunno what you've been up to, visiting my wife this late.'

'You're Lidney,' Gently said.

'Yes, I'm Lidney,' the man said.

'It isn't so late,' Gently said. 'It's about the time Harry French got here on Tuesday.'

The humpty man looked at Gently, puckered eyes,

squashed nose. His head was back in his humpty shoulders, his long body weaved a little on the short splayed legs.

'What do you mean,' the humpty man said, 'come here talking to me like this? Harry French has never been near this place. You'd better watch what you're saying, hadn't you.'

'Harry French came here on Tuesday,' Gently said. 'Some time after ten p.m. he came here. He came here looking for his son who was with you. He didn't like his son associating with you. Also his son was coming into some money and Harry French had suspicions about where it might go to. Tuesday was the day his son should have got the money. He didn't get it. I don't think he was going to get it. Harry French came here that night to blow the set-up apart. He wound up in the river with a hole in his skull about the size of the knob on the bent arm of this doorstop.'

The humpty man came a step closer. 'Say it,' he said, 'say it mate. I'll bloody sue you for defamation that's what I'll do about you. I wasn't trying to pinch young French's money nor Harry French didn't come up this way. Nor nobody didn't kill him with our doorstopper, that got bent being hulled about.'

'Yes, it was hulled about,' Gently said. 'There's marks of that on the lino. There's also marks of a struggle and they haven't been there very long.'

'Didn't I tell you why?' Mrs Lidney said.

'You gave me an explanation,' Gently said. 'I shall have underestimated your husband if he didn't hear it through the keyhole.'

'You lousy sod,' Mrs Lidney said.

'You're a nice bugger aren't you?' the humpty man said.

'What I want to know,' Gently said, 'is how you're putting pressure on young French now.'

The humpty man weaved, crouched his head lower in his shoulders, pushed it up close towards Gently.

'Don't speak to me like that mate,' he said, 'or I'll down you, cop or no cop. You come here insulting my wife, now you're insulting me. You'd just better watch your trap, you had, we're not scared of your sort in these parts.'

'But I've got the doorstop tonight,' Gently said.

'What's that,' the humpty man said. 'What's that about a doorstopper?'

'You threw it at French,' Gently said. 'It grazed his shoulder, didn't down him. He was facing you then. Later on he had his back turned.'

The humpty man's eyes were like needles. He twisted his body, his arms swinging. The smell of Mrs Lidney's cloves and perspiration came strongly. The Cakewalk thumped downriver, it was the only sound from outside. The humpty man's lips were turned in so that his mouth was a seam.

'John French won't be bringing the money,' Gently said. 'That's finished. You won't be touching any money of his. I know he was here, that's the hold you had on him. I don't think he killed his father. I spend my life meeting killers.'

'You filthy pig,' Mrs Lidney shouted.

'You do what, you do what?' the humpty man said.

'I meet killers,' Gently said. 'All shapes and sizes of killers. That's why I'm on this job, I've got a nose for them. Their lies, their threats, their silly mistakes. They make a pattern, an unoriginal pattern, you get to learn it after a time. It doesn't vary, the motive's the same. A killer's alone and he's afraid.'

'Shut up, shut up,' Mrs Lidney shouted.

'Alone and afraid,' Gently said. 'He's playing at innocence and he daren't relax because there's nobody who won't betray him.'

'If you say I did it,' the humpty man said.

'Just throw the sod out, Sid,' Mrs Lidney shouted.

'If you call me a killer,' the humpty man said.

'Yes, if I call you one,' Gently said.

'Throw him out, throw him out,' Mrs Lidney shouted.

The humpty man drew back a little from Gently. His pointed eyes stared at Gently's chest. He kept lifting and dropping his hands like a wrestler shaping to take a hold.

'You lousy bugger,' he said, 'lousy bugger.'

'I'll rip his bloody eyes out,' Mrs Lidney said.

'I've never killed anyone,' the humpty man said. 'Come in here, telling me that. You're another one thinks he can do what he likes with me. Kick me about. Say what you like. Well nobody can do that to me I tell you, I don't give a frig who they are.'

'Not me or Harry French either,' Gently said.

'I don't care who they are,' the humpty man said.

'Calling you a swindler maybe, a pimp,' Gently said. 'In front of your wife and John French. Giving you the sack.'

'Why don't you bash him one Sid?' Mrs Lidney said.

'I'll bash him one yet,' the humpty man said.

'The way you bashed Harry French,' Gently said. 'On Tuesday night. Right where we're standing.'

'He wasn't here,' Mrs Lidney screamed. 'How many more times, it's a load of bull.'

The humpty man stared at Gently's chest, swung his hands, didn't say anything.

'It'll come out,' Gently said. 'Nothing will stop it coming out. We've tracked him through the bridge to the rond, from the rond to this hallway. This is where he had the fight that left the marks on his body. Perhaps he died in this hallway. We'll find that out too.'

'You can't find it out,' Mrs Lidney shouted. 'You bloody well can't.'

'Shut your mouth Rhoda,' the humpty man said.

'Or if he was followed outside,' Gently said, 'whichever way, we'll find out. It'll take a few hours longer if you stick to your lies, that's all.'

'You think you're clever,' the humpty man said.

'We don't need to be clever,' Gently said.

'You aren't clever at all,' the humpty man said. 'You'll find that out. You aren't clever. If I get you into court you won't look clever, you'll look the lousy frigger you are.'

'It's a risk,' Gently said. 'I'll try not to lose sleep over it. That's not the advice I'd give you. I'm taking this doorstop away with me.'

'Oh and are you?' the humpty man said.

'Yes,' Gently said. 'Any objections?'

The humpty man looked at him intently.

'Here's your receipt,' Gently said.

He set down the doorstop, took out his notebook, scribbled a receipt, shoved it in the man's hand. The man looked at the receipt, threw it on the floor. The woman stooped and picked up the receipt. Gently took the doorstop and pushed past the man. The man staggered. Nobody said anything.

Also on this night of August 7th when Superintendent Gently was returning along the cinder path being abreast of the rond where the shred of nylon was found his eye was caught by a small bobbing flame on the other bank of the river and Reuben's Cakewalk being by that time silent he heard a faint hiss after the flame was extinguished. Thus Superintendent Gently halted and stared very hard across the river and advanced to the dyke under the Speltons' fence in which three of the Speltons' dinghies lay moored. He took the outermost dinghy and rowed it across the slow flood and in the well of the old houseboat moored opposite he found a man smoking a pipe and ledger fishing. As the dinghy drew close the man said:

'Do you watch out for my line down there.'

'I can see your line,' Gently said.

'Well keep your oar out of it,' the man said. 'What do you want, you're not a bailiff. You've just pinched one of Speltons' dinghies.'

'I'm a policeman,' Gently said.

'Oh, ah,' the man said. 'I get you now.'

Gently shipped his oars, let the dinghy touch, took hold of the gunnel of the houseboat. The man who was fishing was a short elderly man and he wore a dark-coloured hat with a sagging brim. He was smoking shag. He was fishing with a short glass rod. The glow of the pipe showed a wrinkled forehead and thick uptilted eyebrows.

'About this Harry French job,' he said.

'Yes,' Gently said. 'You're the owner of this house-boat?'

'Blast yes of course,' the man said. 'I'm Billy Stratton, that's who I am.'

'Were you here on Tuesday?' Gently said.

'Yes I was here Tuesday,' the man said. 'But I didn't stir out of the old boat, so I didn't see nothing worth talking about. I live at Starmouth you know, I come here nights now and then. Too much traffic in the daytime. I get a little fishing in the evening.'

'You were fishing on Tuesday evening?' Gently said.

'From about eight o'clock time,' Billy Stratton said. 'Till Reuben packed up, it was slow on Tuesday. All this close weather don't do it any good.'

'Do you know young John French?' Gently said.

'I knew his father,' Billy Stratton said.

'Did you see John French on Tuesday?' Gently said.

'Not as far as I know,' Billy Stratton said.

'Did any yachts go by? A half-decker?'

'Can't say I'd remember,' Billy Stratton said. 'There was a lot of these, spiv-boats, I call them, those hire launches that make the wash. Then there was a banana-boat, that's a trip-boat, and cruisers any amount. But I did see Harry French, couldn't have been a long while before.'

'When?' Gently said.

'Oh sometime after ten,' Billy Stratton said. 'Not long before I packed up he came creeping up here. Of course it might not have been him, he didn't have any lights on, but anyway it was his launch and I thought it was him when he got out. Just over there where you came from. He looked this way, but he wouldn't have seen me.'

'After that how long were you fishing?' Gently said.

'Till Reuben finished,' Billy Stratton said. 'He's finished now, about half past ten. Then I brewed some cocoa and turned in on the bunk.'

'Did you see or hear anything after that?' Gently said.

'Not once I'm in kip,' Billy Stratton said. 'I'm like the Seven Sleepers when I'm aboard the *Penelope*, you could let off an atom bomb and I wouldn't hear it. He moors up, stands there a bit. He was looking around, listening. Then he mooches away up the path. That's about all I can tell you.'

'Up the path,' Gently said.

'Why yes,' Billy Stratton said, 'up the Sounds way.'

'Thanks,' Gently said. 'Where can I find you again?'

'Thirty-seven South Quay Row,' Billy Stratton said.

Gently said: 'Tomorrow morning I'd like you to make a statement of what you've told me. If you'll go to the County Police Headquarters in Trafalgar Road they'll take your statement there.'

'Blast I'd have been before,' Billy Stratton said. 'I didn't know I'd seen anything special.'

'If you will,' Gently said. 'How's the fishing tonight?'

Billy Stratton laid down his rod, felt for a string that

hung from the gunnel. He pulled on the string. A wobbling keep-net came out of the water with splashings and slitherings.

'Do you strike a match,' Billy Stratton said.

Gently struck a match, held it to the net. About a couple of stone of biggish bream were flapping and writhing at the bottom of the net. Their fish smell was heavy. The brown mesh of the net was coated with their slime. Most of them were around the pound mark but several would have scaled two or three.

'What do you think,' Billy Stratton said. 'There's some rum old bream there, aren't th'?'

Gently nodded. 'Some rum old bream,' he said.

'I got amongst them,' Billy Stratton said.

Thus and finally on August 7th Superintendent Gently rang County Police Headquarters and requested a photographer and two men else and a van to carry a roll of lino and a drill and a saw to cut out a section of plasterboard and a certain instrument of authorization and notice to technical personnel who might otherwise have been off duty and asleep. All of which requests were expedited.

CHAPTER SEVEN

I NSPECTOR PARFITT DROVE into Haynor and it was the
morning of Saturday August 8th. Because Inspector
Parfitt was a local man he knew what to expect at
Haynor and he found what he expected. He found first
a stream of traffic not to say a jam which halted him a
long time at the bridge but which treated him to the
sight which he always enjoyed of Reuben's Cakewalk
being dismantled: Reuben having done with Haynor for
a twelvemonth and in early train to remove to
Wrackstead. He found secondly about the yards and
about the car parks and open space adjacent to the yards
a large busy population wearing slightly crumpled city
clothes with on their faces expressions of irritation and
anxiety and in their hands crammed luggage packed
fishing rods even tennis rackets and frogman flippers
moving transporting inquiring packing calling swearing
nagging queuing at toilets queuing in the café queuing
to drag luggage on to overfilled buses waiting for hire
cars that didn't arrive and waiting to extract private
cars which were temporarily unextractable. He found

thirdly a species of marine charlady in active possession of the moored craft winkling out reluctant hirers who had not packed overnight and causing an opening and shutting of suitcases on the quays: village ladies of character and energy who shook blankets whisked off sheets rattled saucepans counted cutlery tossed out tins dustpanned out fluff and loudly advised each other of their discoveries and theorized keenly on the basis of them. He found fourthly a team of technicians equipped with toolbags and paintpots and varnish pots and lengths of raw greyish-pink mahogany and brass screws and mastick who with much hammering sawing drilling planing shaping fitting swearing dressing screwing caulking painting varnishing arguing and incidental comment were making good the minor bashings stovings rakings grindings hackings bruisings and raspings inflicted by the hirers who held it as an article of faith what they had read in the letting agent's catalogue namely that anyone who could drive a car could drive a twenty-ton motor-cruiser without brakes (though along with three or four thousand other powercraft in one hundred and fifty miles of narrow waterway). He found fifthly a quadruple impingement of evacuees from the bungalows treading their four cinder paths for the last time adding their luggage to the pool of heaps of luggage themselves to the queues their voices to the general voice: and sixthly a number of early-rising night-driving Jones-pacing newcomers arrived heavy-eyed but hopeful but now somewhat silent and in amaze. He did not find William Archer and David Spelton who were superintending the filling out of insurance claims in their respective offices nor easily a place to park his car though it was recognizably a police car. The sun however was shining hotly on the totality of these transactions the empty river moved towards the Sounds a few village people stood watched. None of which surprised Inspector Parfitt or suggested abstract ideas to him. Along with Detective Constable Joyce he entered the Country Club and inquired at the desk for Superintendent Gently.

'Well,' Superintendent Gently said.

'I've brought a warrant for the arrest of the Lidneys with me,' Inspector Parfitt said.

'Have you?' Gently said.

'It's as good as that,' Parfitt said. 'I was waiting for a copy of the lab report or I'd have been out here sooner.'

'You're soon enough,' Gently said. 'I've only just finished breakfast. I don't burn the candle so much these days. Anyway there's no rush. What does the lab report say?'

'I've got it here,' Parfitt said, fumbling his breast pocket.

'No,' Gently said. 'You tell me, it's too early for that sort of handwriting. Any luck with the doorstop?'

'Actually, not much,' Parfitt said. 'It's clean. They must have wiped it, done a pretty good job. All we got off it was a thread of wool that was jammed in that shell pattern at the base. French was wearing a light tweed jacket and the thread matches, but we can't swear to it.'

'When he was hit on the shoulder with it,' Gently said.

'Yes, that's pretty certain,' Parfitt said. 'Our patholo-gist reports that the edge of the shell pattern would cause a graze like the one on French.'

'What about the knob and the fracture?' Gently said.

'Yes,' Parfitt said, 'that's a fit. There's nothing to give complete identification of course, not like breech marks or rifling, but it fits all right. It would make that size and pattern of fracture.'

'No hair, impacted skin?'

'No,' Parfitt said, 'it was wiped.'

'And put back by the door,' Gently said.

Parfitt looked at Gently.

'Go on,' Gently said. 'It just occurred to me that the river was handy. But you meet a frugal murderer now and then. No doubt the doorstop was part of the old home.'

'But I thought Lidney was our chummie,' Parfitt said.

'Yes, that's all right,' Gently said. 'You'll get to know how I work eventually. What did they find on the lino?'

'Blood,' Parfitt said, unfolding the report form. He pointed to some writing on it, said: 'That's it, blood.'

'Whose group?' Gently said.

'Not French's,' Parfitt said. 'Human blood, not French's. Had some ptyalin mixed with it.'

'Good for French,' Gently said. 'He must have copped Lidney in the mouth. I'd say Lidney was getting the worst of it when he picked up the doorstop. Whereabouts was the blood sited?'

'Nearer the front door end,' Parfitt said.

'Yes,' Gently said, 'it fits the picture. Lidney would have backed up there after French entered. So they fight, he's getting the worst of it, he's hit in the mouth and spitting blood. He looks for a weapon, finds the doorstop, throws it, it grazes French's shoulder, falls, bounces. But that wouldn't stop French, he comes up the hallway after Lidney. Lidney hasn't got a weapon now. The doorstop's behind French at the other end of the hallway. So what happens?'

'The devil,' Parfitt said. 'It was someone else who crowned French.'

'Someone entered by one of the doors behind him,' Gently said. 'They picked up the doorstop and felled him with it. Someone a good deal shorter than French if our experiment with the hammer has a bearing. Like Mrs. Lidney. Like John French. It probably lies between those two.'

'The devil,' Parfitt said again.

'Those two,' Gently said. 'And for my money Rhoda Lidney picked up the doorstop. It fits the rest of the facts better. Except for one we'll come to in a minute, when we've done with this line.'

'But hell, it isn't a line,' Parfitt said. 'This is what happened, it must be this. It stands to reason, Lidney didn't have the doorstop, it finished up behind French. French was hit from behind.'

'All right,' Gently said, 'let's go on. French is dead, he's lying in the hallway. He's a sixteen-stone corpse and they can't get a car down the cinder path.'

'A boat,' Parfitt said, 'they put him in a boat.'

'Was there a boat there?' Gently said.

'His own launch,' Parfitt said. 'They'd only to fetch it round to the bungalow.'

'Yes,' Gently said, 'but how did they know about it? How did they know French had come in his launch? How did they know where he'd moored the launch? Unless he'd let it out himself somehow.'

'But it must have been a boat,' Parfitt said. 'They couldn't have carried him down the cinder path. And they wouldn't have slung him into the river off the front, it was too close, he might just have stopped there.'

'So,' Gently said, 'we'll give them the launch. They've brought the launch, got the body into it. What's to stop them from taking it a mile downstream, why do they tip it in so near home?'

Parfitt stared with hooked-up eyebrows. 'The bridge,' he said. 'They wouldn't want to go under it. There'd still be traffic, people going over it, might've been the local copper standing on it.'

'So why not upstream?' Gently said.

Parfitt hesitated longer. 'I wouldn't know,' he said. 'Unless they were planning to make it look like an accident, wanted to keep it close by the yard.'

Gently said to Joyce: 'Have you any ideas, Constable?'

'No sir,' Joyce said. 'I'm afraid I can't figure it, sir.'

'That makes two of us then,' Gently said. 'After we've got him dead I can't figure it either.'

'But damn it,' Parfitt said, 'there must be a way. It was all laid on, the boat, the river. It's all tidied up apart from a detail. We don't know how their minds worked. Perhaps they were trying to put it on the Speltons.'

'Perhaps, perhaps,' Gently said. 'I'm still in the hallway with the body. Or maybe the body's still on his feet and nobody's come out to pick up the doorstop. Or

137

maybe somebody's come out but not to pick up the doorstop, only to break up the rough-house, to try to talk to them. And they did talk and French walked out of that bungalow and the doorstop was put back beside the door.'

'You're not serious,' Parfitt said.

'Yes I'm serious,' Gently said.

'But then how was he killed with the doorstop?' Parfitt said.

'That's it,' Gently said. 'How was he killed with the doorstop?'

Parfitt stared a long time.

'Did you heft the doorstop?' Gently said.

'Yes,' Parfitt said. 'It would kill an elephant. I could kill an elephant with that doorstop.'

'How did you hold it when you hefted it?' Gently said.

'Well, by the shank,' Parfitt said. 'Just below the stock, in the bight of the cable.'

'So as to make a club of it,' Gently said.

'Yes,' Parfitt said, 'a club.'

'You didn't hold it by the base,' Gently said, 'not by that irregular shell pattern where the weight is.'

'Well,' Parfitt said, 'no.'

'Yet that's what we're supposing,' Gently said. 'That somebody did just that. Took an awkward hold on the heavy end of the stop and fractured French's skull with the light end. But that's impossible. I tried it. You can't get the weight of the stop behind the blow. It's like holding a vice with a hammer in it and trying to knock in nails with the hammer. The inertia of the weight is against you, it takes the power out of the blows.'

Parfitt kept on staring. 'All right,' he said, 'then it was thrown. It was thrown once, it could be thrown again. Somebody picked it up and threw it.'

'But the same thing applies,' Gently said. 'You couldn't get the weight behind one of those knobs. If one of them struck anything it would merely spin the stop round, it's only the base that can do any damage.'

'But the stock was bent,' Parfitt said. 'It could fall on the stock hard enough to bend it.'

'Yes,' Gently said, 'by falling on the stock at an angle. Not by falling on the flat face of the knob. We're dealing with a completely round fracture, the weal in the lino is semi-circular. Not by wielding, throwing or dropping the stop can you produce the sort of fracture that killed Harry French.'

Parfitt got up. They were in the Country Club manager's office. Parfitt walked over to the window, looked out at the scene. Two red double-decked buses were filling up opposite the window, the sun fell through the window, the sun was hot. Parfitt stood some moments in the sun watching the buses filling up. Then he turned, came back to his chair, sat. He said:

'So we're back where we started from are we? No arrests, no weapon, nothing to show. I can tear up this warrant and throw it in the river. And give the Lidneys their lino back and apologize for cutting a hole in their wall.'

Gently shrugged, got out his pipe, filled the pipe, lit it, broke the match. 'Yes, it's disappointing,' he said. 'At one time I thought we had a case there.'

'But there is a case there,' Parfitt said. 'Hell's bells,

139

there is a case. French went to the bungalow, there was violence, we know why, we can sew it up. I don't give a damn about the bloody doorstop, let them fight that out in court. I know the way the jury will see it. There's a case, let the Lidneys answer it.'

Gently puffed. 'Stop thinking about juries,' he said. 'First you've to convince the public prosecutor. You've got to tell him things you can't prove.'

'What can't we prove?' Parfitt said. 'We can prove enough to tie it up. So some of it's circumstantial, what does it matter? How can it be anything else?'

'You can't prove,' Gently said, 'that French was ever in the bungalow. You can't prove his son was there. You can't prove he had reason for seeking his son there. Those are the points in chief in the case against the Lidneys and until you can prove one or more of them it's no use taking the case to the public prosecutor. All we can show is that French was near the bungalow, that there are signs of a recent struggle in the bungalow, that John French's alibi is improbable, and that he may have had some trouble with his inheritance. None of which would get a conviction if it was ever aired in a court.'

'Hell, hell,' Parfitt said. He raised a hand. 'Wait a minute,' he said. 'That bit about John French's inheritance – we can lay that on the line.'

'How?' Gently said.

'Laskey and Laskey, the solicitors,' Parfitt said. 'They can tell us what Harry French was up to, that'll be one of your points proved.'

Gently puffed.

'Well, won't it?' Parfitt said.

'The operative word is *can*,' Gently said. 'No doubt the solicitors can tell us, but I can think of no reason why they will.'

'But damn it, this is a murder case,' Parfitt said.

'That's just the objection,' Gently said. 'Their late client is deceased, but their present client is implicated. It's a nice professional question where their loyalty ought to lie, but dead clients don't write cheques. I imagine they'll consider their information privileged.'

Parfitt got off his chair again.

'Still, have you got their number?' Gently said.

'It'll be no use,' Parfitt said. 'I know Herbert Laskey, I play golf with him. If there's a reason for being awkward you've picked the man to be awkward.'

'Yes,' Gently said, 'but French may have filed an injunction. That's a matter of record, they'll have to tell us that.'

Detective Constable Joyce looked up the number. Gently dialled. They waited. Gently introduced himself to the telephone, asked for Herbert Laskey, waited. Then he said:

'Yes good morning. It's to do with the death of Harry French. We think you have some information which may be of use to us. Relating to the late Mrs French's estate. I want to know if you can give me that information. Not over the phone, I can call round.'

Time passed. Gently said:

'Yes indeed. Of course. Yes. Then perhaps you can save me time on a matter of record. Have you lately filed an injunction for Harry French?'

Time passed. Gently said:

'No thank you. That's all.' He hung up, made a face at Parfitt. 'What's Laskey's handicap?' he said.

'There wasn't an injunction,' Parfitt said.

Gently shook his head. 'It was an outside chance. From our talk I should guess there was one pending but none was filed. So that's dead.'

'Then where do we go?' Parfitt said. 'If this isn't good enough we've come to a wall. We know what we know but we can't prove it and there are no angles. So where do we go?'

'It's a stage,' Gently said. 'At this point we go on making motions. Keep leaning. Go and lean on Lidney. Keep putting him through it and putting him through it.'

'You want me to do that?' Parfitt said.

'Yes,' Gently said, 'I want him softened.'

'That's me,' Parfitt said. 'I'd soften rhinoceros hide. That's just my mood. I'd soften a steamroller.'

Thus: while Inspector Parfitt and Detective Constable Joyce went to interview Sid Lidney Superintendent Gently relit his pipe and strolled across to French's yard. He went nowhere particular in the yard and he spoke or sought to speak with no one but he glanced occasionally at the lazy house flag and once at the river which was sleepily flooding. The flag was lifting only at the leech and the leech pointed southerly across the river but every so often the leech flickered westerly and the bulk of the flag rippled and swayed: so that a yacht creeping up on the flood was now winded now unwinded with her main sheet sometimes dripping clear sometimes trailing in the water. Gently also watched this yacht. It

142

took a long time to reach the quays. When it turned up to moor it was headed directly and lost all way and needed quanting in. The name *Brownie 2* was carved in its transom and below the name Starmouth and the initials of a club. It was sailed by a bearded man. He had no crew. Gently went over to the quay. The man glanced at him. Gently said:

'Slow work this morning.'

'Yes,' the bearded man said, 'the wind's flukey.'

'Getting a bit of east in it,' Gently said.

'It'll be a tack up to Marsey,' the bearded man said.

'Will it take you long?' Gently said.

'Hmn,' the bearded man said, snatching with his head. 'I'll be using the motor. I've a seagull in the forepeak. Unless the wind freshens. Which it won't.'

'Is it a tack to Hickstead?' Gently said.

'Not down the broad,' the bearded man said.

'How long would it take to sail to Hickstead?' Gently said.

'Quanting or sailing?' the bearded man said.

'Just sail alone,' Gently said.

'Well,' the bearded man said, 'you might make it by teatime, if you had enough patience. But if the tide turns before you cross the Sounds you won't make it at all. You going for a sail?'

'I'm thinking of it,' Gently said.

'Well, take a quant with you,' the bearded man said, 'or better still take an outboard.'

'Would you describe the wind as a light variable north-easterly?' Gently said.

'In polite society,' the bearded man said, 'provided

you're using capital letters. Provided the capital letters are italics and a foot high and painted with dayglo. Otherwise you'd describe it as a bloody stinker and be guilty of crass understatement.'

'Thank you,' Gently said. 'I just wanted an opinion.'

'I'm two hours out from the Lion dyke,' the bearded man said, 'and that's my opinion in a nutshell.'

He turned, began getting sail off. Gently nodded, left the quay. The leech of the house flag was plucking westerly but without strength to pull the bunt after it. Gently crossed the yard to the waste ground behind it where the *Kiama* lay black among her oil drums. The *Kiama* looked tinder-dry under the sun and the seams gaped along her length. Gently stood, watched the *Kiama*. Behind the *Kiama* was a rusted wire fence. Behind the fence was rough marsh. On the rough marsh something moved. Gently passed by the *Kiama*, skirted nettles, ducked under an elder bush, came to the fence. He found a gap in the fence, scrambled through the gap, pushed through some bush willows, came to a small clearing. In the centre of the clearing was a primitive hut. The hut was made of old barrel staves and thatched with marsh litter. In front of the hut were the ashes of a wood fire enclosed by a rectangle of stones and old bricks and beside it a fire-blackened tin and a heap of dried alder twigs and a wooden-handled padsaw with Spelton branded on the wooden handle. And in the hut itself squatted Vera Spelton dressed in jean trousers and a sleeveless cream blouse. Her blue eyes were fixed without expression on Gently until he stopped in front of her. Then they smiled. She said:

'He's in the *Kiama*, you know.'

Who is in the *Kiama*?' Gently said.

'Him,' Vera Spelton said. 'The one you want. Him. Him.'

'Do you mean John French?' Gently said.

'The one you want,' Vera Spelton said. 'He's in the *Kiama*. I watched him go in. You can get him now and take him away.'

'What makes you think I'm going to take him away?' Gently said.

'Yes,' Vera Spelton said. 'You're going to take him away. I know. Because he did something awful, I know all about it. I've been keeping an eye on him for you. You can take him away now.'

She smiled with great brilliance.

'He's the one,' she said. 'He was there that night, I know, I saw him, I'll tell the judge I saw him if you like.'

'I see,' Gently said. He looked about him, found a barrel stave, squatted on it. 'I expect you've kept an eye on him a lot,' he said.

Vera Spelton nodded briskly. 'I keep an eye on them,' she said. 'I know all the things that go on. I've got my secret places for watching them. Shall I tell you what I know?'

'Why not?' Gently said.

'Well I know about him and that woman,' Vera Spelton said. 'The woman who attracts them so much, though she isn't half so attractive as I am. But she doesn't play fair. I keep my clothes on you know. That woman takes her clothes off, it's the only way she can attract them. And she's terribly naughty you know, you wouldn't believe if I told you, she does the very naughtiest things. Don't you take them away for that?'

'No,' Gently said, 'not precisely for that.'

'Well she doesn't play fair,' Vera Spelton said. 'I should take her away if I were you. And she'd been naughtiest of all with him? I don't mind telling the judge about that. I think she gives him something funny to drink, otherwise he'd never let her do such things.'

'Have you ever attracted him?' Gently said.

Vera Spelton pouted. 'I haven't tried,' she said. 'No, I'm certain I've never tried. But I could do. If that would help you to take him away.'

'Why do you want me to take him away?' Gently said.

'Oh I don't care,' Vera Spelton said. 'I don't mind a bit about that. Except it makes Jackie and Dave so funny.'

'Hmn,' Gently said.

'Shall I tell you some more?' Vera Spelton said.

'Tell me about Tuesday night,' Gently said.

'Oh nothing happened that night,' Vera Spelton said.

'Nothing happened on Tuesday?'

'No,' Vera Spelton said. 'The man was there, you know, her husband. She's never naughty till he goes out. Then they go into the room at the back with the bed and she locks the door and he lies on the bed. But not on Tuesday. The man was there. When he didn't come out I didn't bother to watch.'

'But he, John French, went there on Tuesday?'

'Yes,' Vera Spelton said, 'I told you so.'

'About what time?' Gently said.

'It was after tea,' Vera Spelton said. 'I saw him, he

146

didn't see me. I was watching in one of my secret places. He came up the river in a dinghy with a motor on it and he tied the dinghy up in the bungalow dyke. But the man was there, I knew that, and he didn't come out as he usually does. So nothing could have happened on Tuesday. I can tell you about some other times.'

'Where's this secret place of yours?' Gently said.

'This is a secret place,' Vera Spelton said. 'I can watch him from here when he's on the *Kiama*. I can creep up to the fence and watch everything.'

'But where's that other secret place?' Gently said.

'Oh I've got all sorts,' Vera Spelton said. 'People don't know my secret places, I'm very clever, they don't know them.'

'How long were you watching there?' Gently said.

'We built the *Kiama*,' Vera Spelton said. 'Our grandfather built it. It's a very fine boat. It won all the races it ever sailed in. I don't know how it got here in this yard. They're nothing to do with us here you know.'

She smiled at Gently. Gently said nothing.

'They can't build boats here,' Vera Spelton said. 'Some yard-hand of Daddy's set up this yard, but I wouldn't advise you to hire a boat here.'

'I thought Harry French built the *Kiama*,' Gently said.

Vera Spelton's smile went blank.

'Yes, the man who was murdered on Tuesday,' Gently said. 'He built the *Kiama*. Harry French.'

Vera Spelton turned pale. Her face worked. She began to bubble saliva and spit. She made sounds. At last she said:

147

'I hate you. I hate you. I hate you, I hate you.'

'I may be mistaken,' Gently said.

'You're wicked, I hate you,' Vera Spelton said.

'It needn't have been Harry French who built the *Kiama*,' Gently said.

'Oh you're a bad man,' Vera Spelton said, 'a bad man. I hate you, I'll never tell you anything again.'

'Yet why shouldn't Harry French have built the *Kiama*?' Gently said.

'He's nobody nobody,' Vera Spelton said. 'There's nobody like that, he's gone, there never was anybody. It's wicked and I hate you. It was grandfather who built the *Kiama*. It's a Spelton boat, you know it is, you're as bad as he was, bad, bad. I hope someone does something awful to you. You're nobody either. Nobody. Nobody.'

'Perhaps I'm like Harry French,' Gently said.

Vera Spelton stared, spitting, crouching.

'Perhaps I drove my launch up to the quay near yours,' Gently said, 'perhaps I went along the cinder path to the bungalow. Perhaps I went into the bungalow and fought the man there. Then perhaps I came out again and went back to my launch. And perhaps you saw it all from a secret place when Jackie and Dave thought you were in bed. And you saw someone come up behind and hit me and you saw me fall into the water and that's why I'm nobody nobody and couldn't have built the *Kiama*.'

She crouched back deeper into the hut. Her chin was tucked in, her face small. Her mouth bubbled, she stared at Gently. The saliva dripped on the front of her blouse.

'Who was it hit me?' Gently said.

She made sounds. She dribbled.

'Someone with a hammer,' Gently said. 'You wanted them to hit me, and they hit me. Was it the man from the bungalow?'

Vera Spelton was silent.

'Was it Jackie, was it Dave?'

Vera Spelton made a whining noise.

'Was it the one who's in the *Kiama*?'

Vera Spelton stopped dribbling. Her eyes flickered, looked slanting at Gently.

'Was it?' Gently said.

Vera Spelton smiled.

'Where were you watching from?' Gently said.

Vera Spelton kept smiling.

'From the top end of the yard, wasn't it?' Gently said.

Vera Spelton kept smiling.

Gently didn't say anything.

Vera Spelton rose, smiling.

'I'm afraid all our boats are let for this week,' she said.

'That's a pity,' Gently said.

'Yes, you'll have to go elsewhere,' Vera Spelton said. 'We're very popular of course. People always come to Speltons first. But actually all our booking is done through Hookers, the agents.'

'I've seen their catalogue,' Gently said.

'So sorry,' Vera Spelton said. 'We may have something later. Why don't you keep in touch with us?'

Gently rocked forward, got to his feet. Vera Spelton didn't stop smiling. She had saliva on her chin and saliva made a dark patch on her blouse. She shook her honey-coloured hair. In the sun it looked like gold wire.

Very fine gold wire. Her hair was very clean and well brushed.

'Was there anything else?' Vera Spelton said. 'Perhaps my brothers can help you.'

Gently said nothing, turned away, went through the bush willows back to the fence. When he came to the fence he stopped. John French was standing on the other side of the fence. John French's face was greyed, his eyes were large, dark. He faced Gently. His eyes were questioning. They stood facing each other for some moments. John French said:

'I, I've talked to my lawyer.'

'What did you tell him?' Gently said.

'It was on the phone,' John French said. 'I didn't say much, only about the alibi.'

'So he gave you advice,' Gently said. 'He told you not to answer *any* more of my questions?'

'Yes,' John French said. 'Not to answer any questions. Not except in his presence. That's what he said.'

The sun beat down.

'Tell me,' Gently said, 'who was it built the *Kiama*?'

John French looked at Gently. 'I don't know,' he said. 'Perhaps she's Brighton's, Billy Brighton's.'

'Not one of Speltons'?' Gently said.

'Not Speltons',' John French said. 'She's too big.' He sank his eyes. 'Vera,' he said, 'Vera thinks she's Speltons'. She thinks a lot of things.'

'Yes,' Gently said. 'Vera.'

John French didn't raise his eyes.

'But she can't go into the witness box,' Gently said.

John French was quite still.

'I suppose,' Gently said, 'your lawyer didn't bar you from sailing.'

'I'm not going sailing,' John French said.

'Oh I think you are,' Gently said. 'You're going to sail that half-decker of yours to the far end of Hickstead Broad and back. The same wind, the same tides, the same distance, the same course. Eleven miles there and back. You tell me it takes four and a half hours.'

'But there isn't as much wind,' John French said.

Gently nodded. 'The same wind. I'll ring Willard and have it confirmed. And you don't need much wind, you can sail, remember?'

'No,' John French said. 'It isn't fair.'

'Come on,' Gently said, 'let's rig the half-decker.'

He got through the fence. He touched John French's shoulder. John French shuddered, followed Gently.

CHAPTER EIGHT

THUS: TOWARDS LUNCHTIME on August 8th John French went to the half-decker mooring and rigged a half-decker while Superintendent Gently rang the local meteorological office and was assured that the wind conditions matched those of Tuesday: also being a provident man Superintendent Gently visited the Country Club where he ordered and was supplied with a wicker lunch-basket and a big vacuum flask. These he carried to the mooring. John French was sitting in the half-decker at the mooring. The half-decker was moored by the bow and was swinging upstream her sail being empty and the tide at flood. She was eighteen feet L.O.A. by six feet six inches by two feet six draught and she was built of dark lustrous red mahogany rails coamings transom all of her. She had an entry between fine and bluff like the solid breast of a gamecock and amidships the slightest tumblehome and a shaling lotus-blossom exit. She was rigged with a balanced lugsail though not the common balanced lugsail this being an aristocrat among lugsails like the sheerly perfect wing of a bird marrying exactly precisely entirely with the intention of the hull the balance the genius of the hull as notes in an immaculate musical chord. The name of the half-decker was *Shakuntala* which is properly pronounced Sha-koon'-ta-lah: Shakuntala the beloved of a Hindu king who was descended from the moon: Shakuntala who swayed the Moon's son who swayed the moon who swayed the waters Shakuntala Shakuntala: so the half-decker was named.

Gently stood looking at the half-decker with its name *Shakuntala*. He said:

'Is she one of your father's boats?'

John French looked at him, tossed his head. 'She's one of the Old Man's boats,' he said. 'My father only built motor-cruisers.'

'No yachts at all?' Gently said.

'No,' John French said, 'no yachts. You can't go wrong building motor-cruisers. As long as they'll float they'll work.'

'What about you,' Gently said. 'Don't you want to build yachts?'

John French looked at the water. 'There's no point,' he said. 'There's no more room here for sail. The Broads have been handed over. Nobody cares. Anything goes. So build cruisers. Take the suckers' money.'

Gently motioned towards the half-decker.

'Take the suckers' money,' John French said. 'Money is all that counts here. Give them the spiel and take their money.'

Gently shrugged, didn't say anything. He handed the basket and flask down to John French. John French stowed them forward next to the tabernacle. Gently looked at his watch. The time was noon.

'This isn't going to prove anything,' John French said. 'Nobody can sail without wind.'

'That's just what we're going to prove,' Gently said. 'Up till now I thought you held a different opinion.'

'Yes, but there was more wind on Tuesday,' John French said. 'I could sail. There was more wind.'

'You can argue it out with Mr Willard,' Gently said. 'For me, you've to be back here by five p.m.'

'It's a damned waste of time,' John French said.

'I'll cast off,' Gently said, 'then you can demonstrate.'

He loosed the painter, pushed the head out, stepped aboard, took a seat to looard. His weight swung the sail out on the port tack but the sail hung slack and slightly wrinkled. They were under the lee of Speltons' sheds and later they would be under the lee of a mile of bungalows. The tops of the willows by the Bridge Inn moved but *Shakuntala's* burgee trailed heavy, still. John French ruddered across to the lee bank. No wind was there either. John French huddled by the tiller, looked at nothing. They inched upstream on the tide.

'There's where your father moored his launch,' Gently said.

'All right,' John French said. 'So it is.'

'He came up here very quietly without lights,' Gently said. 'But the man in that houseboat saw him. He saw him moor, turn up the path to the bungalow.'

'Oh you've got it all taped,' John French said.

'There was a light in the Speltons' sheds,' Gently said. 'You can see them watching us. Perhaps they were watching then. Vera Spelton, she was watching. She saw an outboard dinghy go upstream.'

'There are dozens of outboard dinghies,' John French said.

'This was a particular one,' Gently said. 'I daresay you'd have seen it too. It came up here at the time you say you set off.'

'Do you think I'm watching all the outboard dinghies?' John French said.

'You'd have plenty of opportunity,' Gently said, 'going upstream at approximately a mile an hour, cursing any wash that knocked the wind out of your sail. This is Saturday lunchtime, we're having it quiet. There'd have been traffic about on Tuesday evening. It wouldn't have helped you to get along. I think you might have noticed that outboard dinghy.'

'Shit on outboard dinghies,' John French said. 'Here's some wind. Watch this.'

Gently looked at his watch. 'Make the most of it,' he said. 'The tide turns around two.'

A draught of warm air filled the sail. It came through the gap above the Speltons' sheds. The blocks ticked as John French drew his sail and *Shakuntala* leaned, accelerated, trilled a ripple under her forefoot. From being asleep she became alive. Her sail curved perfectly and without wrinkle. A silent compression wave slid from under her transom and left no eddy on the flat surface. For two or three seconds she sailed thus before the draught of warm air thinned and collapsed. Then the wrinkles crept back into the sail and the reef points tapped it and she leaned no more and her music died.

She slept. John French breathed hard. He drew on the sheet. *Shakuntala* slept. They had sailed perhaps thirty yards. They were drifting again, empty-sailed.

'She's a pretty boat,' Gently said.

John French looked at Gently, cuddled the tiller.

'If any boat would do it she would,' Gently said. 'I mean sail without wind, the way you're claiming.'

John French said: 'We aren't through yet. When we get past the bungalows, you'll see.'

'But we've only just come to them,' Gently said. 'We aren't up to Lidney's. Where your father was going.'

'Just let me sail, will you?' John French said.

'I still think you need some wind for it,' Gently said.

There was no more wind. Everything was still. The sun beat flashing on the yellow-brown water. The lawns of the bungalows were deserted and there was no other river-traffic nor even an angler on the bank nor a bird nor a cloud in the sky. At the bungalow quays lay launches and rowboats of ugly design and rough maintenance. Silent. Weed growing at their waterlines. Sun spangling their bruised paint. Fishing rods lay neglected with lines and floats dragging upstream and cheap garden furniture stood abandoned and air simmered above felt-tiled roofs. Foot by foot *Shakuntala* crept by them. She was more silent than the river. Her looped sheet hung an inch above the surface and the surface moved equally with the sheet. She drew abreast of Lidney's bungalow. The door and windows of the bungalow were closed. In the cutting beside the bungalow had collected green scum a waterlogged tin the rind of a melon. John French didn't look at Lidney's bungalow. John French scowled and stared upstream. Wind feathered a willow which grew beside Lidney's bungalow but the wind didn't reach *Shakuntala's* sail.

'That's where the dinghy was moored,' Gently said.

John French kept scowling upstream.

'Your father would see the dinghy of course,' Gently said. 'Light from the sitting-room window would fall on the cut.'

'Can't you leave me alone?' John French said. 'Don't you think I have any damn feelings?'

'Don't show them without your lawyer's permission,' Gently said. 'You've shown none so far. Don't start now.'

'Oh God,' John French said, 'I'd like to get out of this. I'd like to get out of it. I'd like to take a plane, fly to Australia. Anywhere would do if it was far enough.'

'But nowhere is far enough,' Gently said. 'A plane wouldn't take you where you want to go.'

'Away from you,' John French said, 'that's far enough.'

'Away from your father,' Gently said. 'It's too far.'

John French turned his head away. *Shakuntala* drifted past Lidney's. A little air came by the next bungalow and the sail rippled but didn't fill. John French twitched the sheet, let it go slack. His chin was tilted down into his chest. The bridge was still so close behind them that they could hear a truck change gear to pass over it.

'You think I hated him,' John French said. 'You can't understand I didn't hate him. But I didn't want him dead, nothing like that, we just didn't get on. That's all.'

'You hated him sometimes,' Gently said.

'I didn't want him dead,' John French said, 'I may have thought about it. What it would be like. But that's not the same. I didn't hate him.'

'Sometimes you'd have liked him dead,' Gently said.

'No,' John French said. 'No. No.'

'It would have made everything so easy for you,' Gently said. 'You'd never had love from him. Him dying didn't matter.'

'He was my father,' John French said.

'He'd never acted like one,' Gently said. 'He'd tried to make a slave of you, that was his being a father. And you were ashamed of him. His character, his principles.'

'But I didn't hate him,' John French said.

'You only wished him dead,' Gently said.

'I did then, I did then,' John French said. 'I wished him dead, all right, but I didn't make him dead. I didn't kill him. I wasn't serious. I didn't hate him really, not hate him.'

'You wished him dead, and he died,' Gently said.

John French closed his eyes. 'What are you trying to do to me?' he said. 'I don't know. What are you after?'

'I'm after the truth,' Gently said.

'That's the truth,' John French said. 'I didn't make him dead. I wanted him dead. I didn't make him dead. That's the truth. But I didn't want him dead either, that's the truth. It's all truth. I don't know what the truth is. I don't think there is any truth.'

'I'll call it truth when it's evidence,' Gently said.

'It can't be evidence,' John French said. 'It doesn't mean anything, none of it means anything. I didn't hate him, didn't want him dead.'

'Then what did you do?' Gently said.

'I,' John French said. He stopped.

'Trim the sail,' Gently said, 'you're missing a puff. Perhaps you'll be lucky and the wind'll freshen.'

John French shortened the sail without looking at it. *Shakuntala* dipped gently, began to travel. John French stared at nothing, eased the tiller aweather, steered, lee'd the tiller as the puff tailed off. Blind ripples from the bow faded out on the surface. The sail slacked, emptied, stilled.

John French said: 'I didn't hate him. I may have thought I did but I didn't. He was my father. I'm like him. He could be decent to me sometimes. He was a swine to me too. That's just how it was. We didn't understand each other. Now he's gone. It's all finished. It doesn't mean anything to say I hated him. That's just how it was, how we were, like that.'

'Yes,' Gently said.

'I'm not blaming him,' John French said. 'Perhaps if I'd been different he'd have been different, I don't know, I didn't want it, I couldn't go to him, we didn't get on. He was a sort of enemy. I had to keep things from him. I didn't want him to know about me. He'd have been against me but even if he wasn't I didn't want that either. And he knew that. He didn't like it. He'd got plans for me. For his son. For his wife's son. I wasn't what he wanted and I didn't want to be, I couldn't help it. My mother was all that mattered to him and she didn't love him, didn't love anyone. I'm sorry he's gone, I'm not sorry about her. I was a stranger to her. She didn't want me.'

159

'Yes,' Gently said.

'She wouldn't have any more after me,' John French said. 'I was an accident. I spoiled her figure. They used to sleep in separate bedrooms. We were beneath her, so was all this, but it was good enough to pay her bills. She really did hate my father, she left her money to me because she hated him. I think she had fancy blokes. He never said anything, she never did wrong in my hearing. I haven't been at home much, Beattie told me things, I saw enough to get the idea. She used to ignore me, didn't want me around. I don't think she fooled him. He was weak, couldn't help it. I'm weak too, I can't help it either. I'm like my father in that. He'd have been all right if he'd had a real wife, if he'd kicked her out, stood alone. She was poison, she was like spilt acid, she made him what he was. He'd have been all right.'

'Yes,' Gently said.

'That was a lot of the trouble, he had to find money for her,' John French said. 'He might have been a craftsman. The Old Man taught him. We had the trade. He could have done what he liked. But he went after the money because he had to because it was the only way to keep her. He never was a craftsman. He was a speculator. He didn't make things. He took money. That's what she did to him, how he was spoiled. Why he'd got a temper. Why he made enemies. Why I was an enemy. Why I hate the business. Why I admire the Speltons. Why I don't care. You're right, damned right, I've wished him dead, I'm one of the reasons why he is dead. Perhaps I'm the real reason why he's dead. Perhaps I killed him. You're damned right.'

'You don't kill by wishing,' Gently said.

'Don't you, don't you?' John French said. 'I wished my mother was dead and she died. Now he's gone too. I killed both of them.'

'You know who killed one of them,' Gently said.

'I, I killed him,' John French said. 'Blame me. Just blame me. I'm the reason he's dead. I don't care.'

Gently didn't say anything. John French was sobbing his breaths. A steadier air was in the sail. *Shakuntala* was quietly treading easterly. The scalloped borders of green reeds were showing at the end of the reach beyond the bungalows and above the flat marsh distances on a sea-paled sky the bleached waves of the sand dunes. The breeze was a sea-breeze. It was coming true. John French was sailing the breeze but not attending to it. John French's eyes were fixed on the water his lips were dry they were dragged at the corners. Gently watched the bungalows, didn't watch John French. *Shakuntala* lisped at her curved forefoot. They passed the pump-mill. They came to the reeds. The reeds were moving swaying rustling. Dragonflies winnowed above the reeds. Small brown birds flickered among the tall stalks. The brown birds chittered. The reeds weaved about them. High over the reeds sailed a round-winged kestrel. On both hands of the river stood the reeds and the river went between and among them.

'You're being lucky with the wind,' Gently said.

John French didn't look at him, didn't say anything. Full-sailed thrusting *Shakuntala* went by the reeds that shivered under the sun. John French's mouth made a tight drooped line. The tiller was loose between his arm and his body. He sailed a line as straight as a crease but never looked where he was sailing. They fetched the turn into Candle Dyke. Into Candle Dyke was a tack. John French began to tack into Candle Dyke but he didn't change sides or glance at his sail. *Shakuntala* tacked. She turned tacks like a dancer. She twisted off tacks, shrugged them away. She climbed the wind in an effortless spiral of darting banks on a flat plane. She came out of Candle into the Sounds. The wind for the Sounds was a close haul. *Shakuntala* fell into the close haul pointing straight and powerful and tight and sheer. John French raised his head to look up the Sounds. The Sounds were a wildness of reeds and water. As John French raised his head the wind faltered, rattled the sail, backed, fell. John French's mouth quivered.

'One hour out,' Gently said.

Shakuntala slowed, lay rocking a moment. The tide was at slack on the Sounds. *Shakuntala* stopped.

'A nice breeze,' Gently said. 'It gave you a lift while it lasted.'

John French licked his lips, swallowed, looked at the burgee, looked at nothing. At the top of the Sounds a yacht was moored. The yacht was small in the distance. A pair of swans rowed across the *Shakuntala*. Nothing else moved except the swans. John French said:

'I could have done what I told you.'

'Your lawyer isn't here,' Gently said.

'Yes I could have done it,' John French said. 'It didn't need a lot of wind, a few puffs like that one. You couldn't prove different. Nobody could. Nobody could swear they didn't see me. Especially after dark they couldn't swear it. All you could do was to tell me I was lying.'

'And of course you were lying,' Gently said.

'You couldn't have touched me,' John French said. 'If it had come to a trial, something like that, they'd have let me off, whatever they thought. It's an alibi. Why shouldn't I stick to it?'

'Keep sailing,' Gently said.

'An alibi,' John French said. 'All I have to do is stick to it.'

He licked his lips with a dry tongue.

'I was at Sid's from about half past six,' he said.

After that John French didn't say anything but sat still and flushed, his mouth trembling. The swans came close and looked at the men and made nasal hisses and dipped their beaks towards the water. Gently looked at John French a long time. One of the swans bit at *Shakuntala*'s rubbing straik. The swans had steady black eyes and mobile heads and continued to make nasal hisses. Gently said:

'So we won't sail down to Hickstead. Perhaps we'd better moor for lunch.'

'I, I don't want lunch,' John French said. 'I can't eat it. I feel sick.'

'Still, you might like some coffee,' Gently said. 'Can we get the boat out of the fairway?'

'There's the boathook,' John French said. 'You can shove on the mud. It's all shallow. We can drop the weight.'

Gently took the boathook, shoved on the mud.

Shakuntala sheered towards the reed-beds. The swans followed. They dipped their beaks at the boathook. John French dropped the weight. The swans backed, hissed. John French touched the halyard, shrugged, sat down again. Gently poured coffee from the flask. John French drank some of the coffee. Gently unpacked the lunch-basket, began to eat. The swans watched Gently. Gently fed the swans. John French said:

'I didn't have the money for Sid.'

Gently said: 'I shall want this taken down and it may be used as evidence. I don't mind waiting till your lawyer's present.'

John French drank coffee. 'I should have had it,' he said. 'I should have had a banker's order from Laskey that morning. About twenty-five hundred. I was going to Starmouth to bank it. It didn't turn up. There was a letter.'

'What sort of letter?' Gently said.

'Oh just a letter,' John French said. 'I've still got it. They referred me to my father. Why I wasn't going to have my twenty-five hundred. So I showed him the letter. And he told me why. That's one of the times I wished him dead.'

'What was his reason?' Gently said.

'He knew about the Lidneys,' John French said. 'He didn't like me being friends with them. He thought they were going to steal the money from me or something. I used to play him up about the Lidneys, he was a snob, I got back at him through them. It was my own fault what happened. That's why I was so mad at him.'

'Yes,' Gently said. 'But what was the truth about Sid and the money?'

John French looked at the coffee beaker. 'It would have been all right,' he said. 'It was a business deal, that's all. Sid and me were going to be partners. He'd got an option on Jimpson's dance hall across the bridge. Peewee Jimpson was his uncle. We'd have made a go of it.'

'Did your father know this?' Gently said.

'No,' John French said, 'not then. He'd just got hold of the idea that I was in something with Sid, I don't know how, we kept it quiet. But it would have been all the same if he did know, he'd have just put a stop to it. He couldn't bear me having to do with Sid. Or Mrs Sid. I told him about that. On Tuesday morning I told him anything, I told him he was a cuckold ten times over.'

'He was seeking an injunction was he?' Gently said.

'Yes,' John French said. 'That's what his game was. I could have fought it, but it would have taken time. The Jimpsons were pushing Sid about the option.'

'So your business deal was done for,' Gently said.

John French hunched himself, twisted the beaker.

'You didn't have the money for Sid,' Gently said. 'And you found Sid wasn't quite such an affable bloke as you'd reckoned.'

John French didn't say anything. He squeezed the beaker till his knuckles blanched. The sun by the reed-bed was blister-hot and heat floated up from the inside of the half-decker. The Sounds were olive glass reflecting sky reflecting reeds reflecting heat. When the swans chukkered the water and lifted their beaks they spilled drops like melted steel drops. John French kept his head down, said:

'There's a lot of things you don't know, can't know. All of a sudden you find that out. You're kidding yourself, you don't know anything. Something happens. Then you find out. Everything's going on round you and it doesn't mean anything only you think it does, you give it a meaning.'

'Yes,' Gently said.

'I'm not going to run Sid down,' John French said. 'I know I was wrong about him. That's nothing. I could be wrong about him again. He's what he is, that's all, nobody can be any different.'

'What is he?' Gently said.

'He's,' John French said, 'I don't know. He's had a lot to put up with, Sid has. Both of them have. He's all right.'

'But he got angry,' Gently said.

John French opened his mouth, checked himself. He finished the coffee left in the beaker, set down the beaker on the side-deck. Gently poured some more coffee into the beaker. John French took the beaker in his hand again. He said:

'I didn't tell Sid right away. I was trying to plan something out. I told Sid I'd be round that evening about the business. I didn't see my father all day. It all made me feel ill. I wanted to get away from them all. I nearly went home and packed a bag. I wish I had. That would have been best.'

'Yes,' Gently said.

'So after tea I went to Sid's place,' John French said. 'They were both there, him and his wife, I think he'd got the idea that something was up. I told them. Sid kept looking at me. He didn't say much at first. Mrs Sid was swearing about my father, saying I could have the law on him for that. Then Sid started on me. It must have been a big disappointment for him. He had to take it out of me at first. He told me he'd trusted me, held me responsible, that it was too late now to back out. He made it seem like I was trying to pull a fast one. I'd never known him like that before. I think it took him a long while to believe that I was telling him the truth. Then he went and stood staring at the wall with his fists doubled, not saying anything. I thought he was going to attack me. His wife, she was scared too.'

John French drank coffee. He said:

'It was Mrs Sid who talked him round. She's got her head screwed on right, they both have in the ordinary way. She said it was no use blinding at me, I wasn't the sort who would welsh on them, we'd better be thinking what we could do rather than calling each other names. She kept on talking to him like that. At last she cooled him off a bit. He came and sat down though he didn't say anything. She made a pot of tea and kept talking. Then he told her to shut up, he was trying to think, and Mrs Sid shut up. She started making up to me a bit instead, told me I couldn't help whose son I was. I didn't like it but she'd calmed Sid down, I just kept quiet, let her carry on. I don't know how long all this took. It was like a dream. It was getting dark. We could hear Reuben's. Then Sid said, well if that was the way it was, I would have to raise a loan on my expectations, he'd told the Jimpsons he'd got the money and the money he'd have to have. I said I'd do anything, I didn't care.

Mrs Sid said she knew I'd stand by my word. Sid said yes, that was the way out, and he knew a loan office in Starmouth who might do the job for me. So I said I'd go there the next day, I'd get the money for him if it killed me, and he said no, I wasn't to take it like that, I'd got to remember it had been a bit of a shock to him. Then he was nice as pie again and Mrs Sid kept coming round me and Sid said he'd better see a man about a dog and Mrs Sid laughed and said we could perhaps manage without him and Sid said he liked his sheets aired. It was just after that we heard the knock.'

John French drank coffee. He said into the beaker:

'We all guessed who it was. I was scared. I think they were. She kept looking at him, he was screwing his eyes up. Then he said my old man better hadn't find me on the premises, they'd put me in the bedroom and lock the door, I'd have to keep right quiet. So I went in the bedroom and they locked the door. I think Mrs Sid went back in the sitting room. Then Sid opened the outside door and it was smashed wide open and there was a scuffle of feet and my father's voice. He was after me, he knew I was there. He was in a terrible sort of passion. At first Sid tried to soothe him a bit but my father was crazy, wouldn't listen. I don't remember much what they said. I don't want to remember. He sacked Sid, called him every name, called his wife names. He was mad. In the end they were fighting. I think my father was getting the best of it. Then Mrs Sid was at the window, told me to get out, I'd have to hide outside, and my father was trying to smash the door down and I jumped out of the window and crawled under the floorboards. They were still fighting. Something hit the floorboards. Mrs Sid must have gone in again. I heard her voice. They unlocked the bedroom. I think my father searched it, looked out of the window. Then they were talking and at last Sid went out and Mrs Sid took my father into the sitting room.'

John French drank coffee. He was trembling. He said:

'I crawled across under the sitting room, the bungalow's on piles off the ground. There's a repair done to the floor there and it's left a gap and I could listen through it. She was trying to get him to see sense. She told him about the Jimpsons and the dance hall. She admitted things about me, tried to make out she was doing him a service. I don't think she knew I was listening, she said things she wouldn't have said. It didn't have any effect. My father was wild, right off his head. She made a sort of pass at him I think, he said something about sooner bathing in a cesspit. Then he went and I could hear her swearing, stamping about the room and swearing, and after I was sure he'd gone I came out and she was still swearing but she was sitting down. I sat down too. I wasn't feeling well. She swore at me, swore at him. It was getting late. Reuben's had finished. I didn't seem to have any strength left. Then Sid came back, I don't know when. He drank some whisky, quite a lot. Mrs Sid calmed down, gave me some whisky, put her arm round me, said she hadn't meant it. I said I'd still go to the loan office. She said yes, she was sure I would. Then I said I'd have to think up a story to tell my father, I wasn't going to admit that I'd been hiding there. Sid didn't say anything at all. He sat in the armchair drinking whisky. I was feeling a bit better. I left, went home in the outboard dinghy.'

'In the outboard dinghy,' Gently said.

John French drank coffee, nodded.

'What did you see?' Gently said.

'I,' John French said, 'I saw my father's launch.'

He held the beaker with both hands because the beaker was shaking. He said:

'I, I nearly ran into it. It was on the right-hand side. It was opposite the Speltons' sheds. It was slantways on, trailing its painter. I pulled up, I could see it was empty, there were lights at Speltons', they may have heard me. It gave me a fright at first, I thought he was waiting for me, then I could see it was adrift. So I went on.'

'And left it there,' Gently said.

'Yes,' John French said, 'I left it, yes.'

'You didn't take it in tow,' Gently said. 'You didn't think it worthwhile to look for your father.'

'But I didn't know,' John French said. 'How was I to know what had happened to him? I wasn't thinking of anything like that, I was thinking he was hanging about trying to catch me. I didn't want anything to do with his launch. I didn't care what happened to it. It had got adrift, that's all I thought about it. I wasn't going to put myself out bringing it in.'

'It didn't strike you as at all significant?' Gently said.

'No,' John French said, 'why should it, I was only too glad he wasn't aboard.'

'Not after the scene at the bungalow, the fighting?' Gently said. 'Sid going out before your father left, coming back to drink, the drifting launch . . . ?'

'No,' John French said, 'no, it's true, my God I didn't think that at the time. I thought about it later but not then. If I'd thought about it then I would have done something.'

'How much later did you think about it?' Gently said.

'Later, later,' John French said. 'When I got to our staithe, when there wasn't a boat there. Even then he might have walked, had his car.'

'I see,' Gently said. 'Go on.'

'That was how it was,' John French said. 'I went home in the dinghy, I thought he'd have taken a workboat, I only hoped he wasn't coming up behind me. But there was nothing at the staithe, nothing coming behind. That's when I started to wonder about it. And if his launch had gone adrift you'd have thought he'd have gone after it, he'd have had plenty of time before I left the bungalow.'

'You might have been expected to think that,' Gently said.

'I did think it,' John French said, 'I'm telling you I did. But he could just have rung the police, come home by road. I didn't know. Not till I went to the house. I expected to find him waiting for me.'

'So he wasn't waiting for you?' Gently said.

'No he wasn't,' John French said, 'He wasn't in the house, not in his bedroom, the door was ajar, I looked in. Then I began to think something had happened, it was midnight, he didn't come. He was in a rage, he might have fallen in. He wasn't a swimmer, he'd have drowned.'

'So naturally you rang us,' Gently said.

'How could I?' John French said, 'how could I?'

'You're certainly on the telephone,' Gently said, 'and the number of the police station is on the front of the instrument.'

'But I'd have had to have told them everything,' John French said.

'You're having to tell it to me now,' Gently said.

'And you're not believing me,' John French said. 'They wouldn't have believed me. They'd have said I killed him.'

'Whereas,' Gently said, 'you say it's Sid who killed him. Though it's only your word against his.'

John French closed his eyes. The beaker was slanted in his hands. Some coffee spilled out of the beaker, over his fingers, on to his knees. He didn't straighten the beaker, didn't brush at the coffee on his trousers. The coffee made stains on the trousers. Gently took the beaker from John French. John French said:

'I, I don't say Sid killed him. That's what you, you're making me say.'

'Is there,' Gently said, 'any other way of interpreting the account you've been giving me?'

'Yes,' John French said, 'Sid didn't kill him. I know he didn't. You'll have to believe me.'

'Then if Sid didn't, you did,' Gently said. 'That's the position we seem to have come to.'

John French swayed his head. 'I've talked to him,' he said. 'He came to me. He brought it up. After the body was found. We talked about it. He didn't see my father again. He knew I was thinking he could have done it.

172

He told me where he went, up the cinder path. I think he was wondering if I'd done it, too. I told him everything. He didn't do it.'

'You've a touching faith,' Gently said. 'You'd better be wrong for your sake. But nobody said your father was killed before you left the bungalow, perhaps you're the better suspect after all.'

John French's lips moved. He didn't say anything.

'He may have kept watch outside,' Gently said. 'He was certain you were there, that you'd come out later. Perhaps the launch wasn't so empty when you found it.'

'He,' John French said. He stopped.

'You know when he was killed,' Gently said.

'I, I don't know anything,' John French said. 'Just what I've told you. I can't tell you any more. I didn't see it happen. I don't know who did it.'

'Yes, that's what you do know,' Gently said.

'No,' John French said, 'no, I don't know. I've told you all I can tell you, it's the truth. Sid'll tell you the same, he didn't know you'd get it out of me.'

'You know who did it and when,' Gently said. 'I've got nothing out of you I didn't have before. It wasn't worth your while to lie any longer so you decided to confess. To put yourself in the clear.'

'No,' John French said.

'You're shopping Lidney,' Gently said.

'Not Sid, not Sid,' John French said.

'Yes, Sid,' Gently said. 'But you're implicated. You must be. You started straight away on your alibi. If you were as innocent as you claim you'd have rung the police, not waked the housekeeper.'

'I couldn't ring the police,' John French said. 'Beattie, I'd thought of that before. If I avoided my father. That was the alibi. To tell him I'd been out sailing.'

'But when your father was missing?' Gently said.

'I, I had to have an alibi,' John French said. 'If something was wrong, if I was asked. He might have come back after all.'

'But you didn't care,' Gently said.

'No, I didn't care,' John French said. 'I do now. I didn't then. He could be dead. I didn't care.'

'So who did it?' Gently said.

John French closed his eyes, groaned.

'If it wasn't Sid,' Gently said, 'it was Dave Spelton.'

John French trembled. He said nothing.

'Yes, Dave Spelton,' Gently said. 'If it wasn't you, wasn't Sid. Your pal Dave. The yachtbuilder. Waiting in the wings with a hammer.'

'Oh God,' John French said.

'You'd cover up for him,' Gently said. 'He's a symbol. He makes these things. Perhaps he had a right to kill your father. Perhaps he came to the door looking for his sister, had the hammer in his hand, saw his enemy standing there on the plot of land, lifted the hammer, squared accounts. That would fit pretty well wouldn't it? Fit the facts. Fit the man.'

'No, not Dave, no,' John French said.

'So,' Gently said, 'who did it?'

'I don't know, I don't know, I don't know,' John French said. 'What's the use of asking me, I don't know. I don't. I don't know.' He opened his eyes suddenly. He rolled them at Gently. 'I'm a liar,' he said, 'a liar, all I've

174

been telling you is lies. I never went to the bungalow at all. I never had a row with my father. I was sailing. I was up here. I was sailing. Sailing. Like I told you all along. The rest is lies. I was sailing.'

'I see,' Gently said. 'I must remember Dave Spelton.'

'Out sailing,' John French said. 'You can't break it. Out sailing.'

He grabbed the coffee beaker, drained it, hurled the beaker up forward. He was shaking like the reeds. He went to the mudweight, lifted the mudweight. He shoved on the reeds with the boathook, came aft, threw himself down by the helm. The ebb was running, *Shakuntala* moved. The swans oared away from them. Gently was silent.

CHAPTER NINE

S O SUPERINTENDENT GENTLY came down from Hay-nor Sounds in the half-decker *Shakuntala* with John French at the helm and no questions asked or answered: very slowly on the ebb tide with a ripple of breeze at rare moments meeting cruisers coming up ugly launches a yacht under power. He disembarked at Haynor bridge. He was more sunburned, perhaps wiser. He said nothing at parting to John French. He carried the lunch-basket and flask into the Country Club. In the lounge of the Country Club he found Inspector Parfitt and Detective Constable Joyce drinking tea, eating toast. He ordered tea and toast from the waitress and joined Inspector Parfitt and Detective Constable Joyce. Inspector Parfitt's face was shiny. He stared at Gently, drank tea, said:

'Do I look the same as I did this morning?'

'Yes,' Gently said. 'Much the same.'

'Well I'm not,' Parfitt said, 'not at all the same. I'm a grinning idiot. Take a look at me.'

'It's been a warm day,' Gently said.

'Not,' Parfitt said, 'only warm. We've had a session,

and man what a session. As from tomorrow I'm chucking police work.'

Gently grinned at Parfitt. 'Snap,' he said. 'Did you soften Lidney for me?'

'Yeah,' Parfitt said. 'Somebody softened somebody, off the cuff I wouldn't like to say who.' He poured more tea, drank more tea. 'I've been brainwashed, threatened and insulted,' he said. 'I'm to be sued for slander, breaking and entering, rape, assault and hell knows what else. Maybe I bashed Harry French myself, I haven't an alibi for Tuesday evening. If you said I did it I wouldn't contradict you. I've got just the hammer in my toolshed.'

'No,' Gently said. 'No phoney confessions.'

'You wouldn't spot the difference,' Parfitt said. 'I've got the details too pat. Let me confess and get it over.'

'I've been out with young French,' Gently said.

'We'll both confess,' Parfitt said. 'I want to get back to the sneak-thieves and double-parkers. I'll murder the next murderer.'

He ate toast, sipped tea. The waitress came with Gently's order. It was the pretty waitress. Parfitt looked at her. Detective Constable Joyce looked at her. Gently poured his tea. The waitress retired. Parfitt sliced a piece of toast.

'Yes,' Parfitt said. 'I don't know who's the chummie, who's the policeman any longer. If they lie like Lidney lies you wind up believing them in the long run. I had to get out of that place. He was breaking me down, him and his missus. I'm not kidding, that's a fact. I was starting to think we'd got it all wrong.'

'That's interesting,' Gently said.

'Oh very interesting,' Parfitt said.

'What were your impressions?' Gently said to Detective Constable Joyce.

'I don't know, sir,' Detective Constable Joyce said. 'He's a queer nut is Sid Lidney. There isn't much I'd put past him. At times I thought we'd got him rocking, other times he seemed quite sure of himself. You'll hardly get him to confess, sir.'

'Don't be funny, Joyce,' Parfitt said.

'Well that's my impression, sir,' Joyce said. 'If he's the chummie he won't confess.'

'He didn't make any admissions,' Gently said, 'nothing about young French, about money.'

'Nix,' Parfitt said. 'Nix again. I couldn't shake them about either.'

'Hmn,' Gently said. 'What do you know of his relatives?'

'I'd say they'll have disowned him,' Parfitt said. 'I believe he's got cousins in the next village, farming people, name of Jimpson.'

'Do they own the dance hall here?' Gently said.

Parfitt shook his head.

'Yes, sir,' Joyce said. 'It belonged to their father. It's been closed since he died. I knew the old man, I used to go there.'

'Well, well,' Gently said. 'Have you finished your tea, Joyce?'

'Yes, sir,' Joyce said, 'just finishing.'

'Take the car,' Gently said, 'go and interview the Jimpsons. Find out what they're intending to do with the dance hall, whether Lidney holds any sort of option on it, whether John French is connected with the deal, whether they're proposing to withdraw the option. Whether there was a date on which Lidney promised payment but defaulted from paying. Just the information, we'll get statements later, don't waste time, bring it back here.'

'Yes, sir,' Joyce said, gulping down toast. 'Details of an option granted to Lidney.'

'With special reference to John French as a backer,' Gently said.

'Yes, sir,' Joyce said, 'I'm with you.' He drank tea, stood up, went.

Parfitt held his toast-knife vertical, took a sight over the tip of the blade. 'Is this what I think it is?' he said. 'You've got chapter and verse for the motive?'

Gently shrugged. 'Joyce is going to find out for me,' he said.

'You screwed this out of young French,' Parfitt said.

Gently said: 'John French came clean, then he withdrew all he'd told me. But he was telling the truth, I had him rubber-legged, he could only hold out on the odd lie. He gave himself and Mrs Lidney an alibi, left Lidney holding the hammer.'

'For that I'll love him,' Parfitt said. 'After that I'll be his elder brother.'

'Only I'm not sure,' Gently said, 'what were the lies he was holding out on. He denies either doing it himself or knowing who did do it, those are the critical lies of the bunch. Which makes you look closer at Mrs Lidney.'

'I still love him,' Parfitt said. 'I'll accept Mrs Lidney and still love him. If I met Mrs Lidney with a hammer in her hand I'd blow a whistle and run like a bastard.'

'French was left alone with Mrs Lidney,' Gently said. 'By John French's account she's the last person to have been with him. Except that John French says different she could have followed him from the bungalow and she was in a murderous mood when he left. She'd let out something he didn't know, what John French was aiming to do with his money. That was a false step. He'd have made her understand that. There was only one way for her to retrieve the situation. And if he knew she'd done it you'd expect John French to cover for her, even to throw Lidney to the wolves if it became a choice. The woman who makes a man of you is a special woman. She may be a Rhoda Lidney, but you wouldn't give her away.'

'So she's the chummie,' Parfitt said.

'No,' Gently said, 'I just don't know. There's so much truth in what John French told me that I can only speculate, starting with the lies. Because there's Dave Spelton too, John French is tender about him. Dave Spelton is what John French would like to be, a man who designs and builds yachts. He's a symbol. French would cover for him. It was my bearing down on Spelton that made French recant. He'd got to the end when I suggested Spelton, all he could do then was retreat to his first alibi.'

'Oh, the devil,' Parfitt said, 'there's no dragging in Spelton at this stage. We're lined up, we're set to go, the Speltons are out, I never did like them for it.'

'But we aren't lined up,' Gently said. 'We're still

playing with three or four suspects. They're covering for each other. They know who did it. That's the situation. We haven't cracked it.'

'But not Spelton,' Parfitt said, 'not in this world, not Spelton. At one time the Speltons were right in the picture, but hell they aren't there any longer. Their grudge is an old one, goes too far back. There's nothing in that angle about French abusing the sister. The Lidneys and the son, that boiled up on Tuesday. It's between those three, doesn't touch the Speltons.'

Gently looked at Parfitt. 'You too?' he said.

'All right, me too,' Parfitt said. 'I'm a local man, I was bred at the riverside, I know how young French would feel about the Speltons. Besides it's common sense to eliminate the Speltons. They were outside of what was going on that night.'

Gently drank tea, cut toast. 'Yes,' he said. 'It's common sense.'

'So what's wrong with common sense?' Parfitt said.

'The Speltons weren't outside it,' Gently said. 'Vera Spelton wasn't outside it. Some part of the time she was acting the spy. I talked to her this morning. She saw the comings and goings, perhaps more than that. She may have been involved, may have involved Dave Spelton. Dave Spelton has a temper, is violent, uses hammers.'

'But Vera Spelton's a nut, you can't believe her,' Parfitt said.

'Her story checks,' Gently said. 'It checks with John French's story, where it touches. Vera Spelton would like me to arrest John French. She fingered him for me this morning. She may have been an eyewitness to the murder, but it doesn't follow that she saw John French do it.'

Parfitt's eyes were round. He said nothing.

'She isn't a fool,' Gently said, 'She's an M.D. but she knows a hawk from a harnser. You liked John French. She fingered him for me.'

'Oh to hell with it,' Parfitt said.

Gently ate some of his toast.

'I still don't go with it,' Parfitt said. 'I don't care. I'll be bloody biased.'

'I'm biased too,' Gently said, 'but mine's a bias towards the facts.'

'Lidney is a fact,' Parfitt said. 'He'll do. He's my bias. He's my fact.'

Gently went on eating, drinking. Parfitt smoked cigarettes. They didn't look at each other. Cars kept arriving, parking outside. Fresh people, fresh luggage spilled out on the parks. The wedge of river they could see was boiling with the wash of outgoing cruisers. A windless sail rocked, flapped, at last was lowered from a jerking mast. More cars arrived, more people. The mast kept jerking. The wash kept boiling. The waitress came, called Gently to the phone. Parfitt smoked. Gently came back. Parfitt said:

'What's the latest in facts?'

Gently shrugged. 'All confirmed,' he said. 'Lidney had the option. It falls in today. He was to have paid up Tuesday, then yesterday. John French was backing him.'

Parfitt stubbed out a cigarette.

'So,' Gently said, 'we'll take him in. Let him cool his heels. Hear what he has to say.'

* * *

The humpty man came into Superintendent Glaskell's office at eight p.m. on Saturday August 8th and he was still dressed in dungarees and a khaki shirt but he wore also an old jacket sagged at the pockets. He was brought into the office by a uniform man who had a hand on the humpty man's arm and the roll or shamble in the humpty man's gait seemed accentuated as he came into the office. All the lights in the office were switched on but especially a floodlight behind the desk. The office was warm, the floodlight was warm, it was also extremely bright. At the desk sat Superintendent Gently. On Gently's right sat Inspector Parfitt. On Gently's left sat Detective Constable Joyce. At a separate table sat a uniformed shorthand writer. In front of the desk stood a low wooden chair which had been fetched into the office from a detention cell. It was a scrubbed unvarnished chair and it stood alone in front of the desk. The uniform man ushered the humpty man to this chair but the humpty man ignored it and remained standing. The floodlight was nevertheless very bright on the humpty man. The uniform man closed the door, stood at ease with his back to it. Gently said:

'You can sit down Lidney.'

'Can I?' the humpty man said. 'Thanks very much.'

He continued to stand. His eyes glittered, small. He was sweating. He smelled of sweat. Gently said:

'You've been brought here, Lidney, to sign a statement about Tuesday evening. You're going to give us your account of Tuesday evening and that account will be taken down in shorthand. But first I'm going to tell

183

you that your account to date doesn't square with certain evidence we've collected. And secondly I have to warn you that you're not obliged to say anything. What you do say will be taken down, may be used in evidence. This is all the warning I'm going to give you. Do you understand what I'm saying?'

The shorthand man scribbled. Lidney looked at the pencil looked at Gently. His big mouth twisted, he said:

'Are you charging me with doing him in?'

'I'll tell you that when I've heard your statement,' Gently said.

'Yes,' Lidney said, 'yes. You're a nice bugger, aren't you?'

Gently didn't say anything. Lidney stood, sweated. The pencil stopped scribbling shorthand. The floodlight buzzed, hissed a little. Lidney said:

'What's this evidence?'

'You'll hear later,' Gently said.

'Oh yes, so you can trap me,' Lidney said.

'I can only trap you in telling a lie,' Gently said.

'And suppose I don't make any statement?' Lidney said.

'That's up to you,' Gently said.

'If someone's accusing me I've a right to know,' Lidney said.

'When they do you will know,' Gently said. 'All we're asking for at the moment is your statement.'

'Why don't you come out with it?' Lidney said. 'Why all this rigmarole if you're going to charge me?'

'Just give your statement,' Gently said.

'Just bloody hang yourself,' Lidney said.

He came up closer to the desk.

'You're going to fix me, aren't you?' he said. 'You've had that stuff out of my bungalow, you can show it in court, that's good enough. So you keep coming at me and coming at me. You think I'll bloody break down and weep. You get me here, pretend to know things, think I'll spew my guts up to you. But you're wrong, I'm the wrong bloke. I was brought up in a different school. If you're going to arrest me, just get on with it. Then we'll see where it gets you.'

'Meanwhile,' Gently said, 'we'd like your statement.'

'No doubt you would,' Lidney said.

'In case it explains our new evidence,' Gently said.

Lidney looked at him, sweated.

'Let's put it this way,' Gently said. 'You've a chance now to tell the truth. You've lied before. We'll forget about that. I wouldn't blame you for lying if you were innocent. But now we know too much about it, I'm not pretending about the evidence. So this is your chance to clear it up, and you'll take it. If you're innocent.'

'You lousy ferret,' Lidney said. 'You're on that tack, are you?'

'If you won't make a statement,' Gently said, 'that way we'll know where we stand too.'

Lidney's mouth twisted, he puckered his eyes, there was sweat on the bald part of his head. The uniform man at the door shifted his feet, looked at his feet, looked at Lidney. Lidney shuffled further towards the desk. He stooped. His humped back looked humptier. He said:

'You've been getting lies out of young French, haven't you?'

185

'I've been making inquiries,' Gently said.

'Yes, out of young French,' Lidney said. 'I thought he wouldn't stand up to you long. Clever buggers aren't you, going after the kid. As though he didn't have enough to put up with anyway. Blinking heroes, that's what you are, nagging at the kid till you got something out of him.'

Gently didn't say anything.

'Heroes,' Lidney said. 'Only you aren't dealing with a kid any longer. And if I don't know what you drove him to say, I don't know what you think I'm going to tell you. Does he say I did it?'

'Did you do it?' Gently said.

'If he does that's one lie,' Lidney said. 'I wasn't far off, I've admitted that, but it wasn't me, nor he couldn't have seen who it was.'

'Why couldn't he have seen it?' Gently said.

'Because he was somewhere else,' Lidney said. 'There, that's evidence, put that down. He was somewhere else, he couldn't have seen it.'

'How do you know?' Gently said.

'Because I know where he was,' Lidney said.

'Then you know when French was killed,' Gently said.

'Didn't know it was a secret,' Lidney said, 'is it?'

'Apparently not to you,' Gently said. 'So now you can tell us. When was he killed?'

Lidney looked at Gently with small eyes. 'When someone copped him with a hammer.' he said.

The shorthand writer wrote shorthand.

'What makes you say a hammer?' Gently said.

'Because it was a bloody hammer,' Lidney said. 'That's why. What his nibs was searching the yard for. Not my doorstopper, a bloody hammer.'

'We don't know it was a hammer,' Gently said.

'Then you're the only ones who don't know it,' Lidney said. 'Every bugger else does.' He winked sweat from his eyes.

'So,' Gently said, 'where were you at that time?'

'Not where I could see it done either,' Lidney said.

'But where were you,' Gently said, 'where John French might think you'd done it?'

'Never mind about young French,' Lidney said.

'Oh yes,' Gently said, 'we'll have to keep him in the picture. He couldn't have thought you'd done it if he'd been on the Sounds in a half-decker.'

'I tell you never mind about him,' Lidney said. 'He was where he was, I was where I was. We didn't neither of us see it done, that's all that matters to you.'

'And you were in the bungalow of course,' Gently said.

'I was,' Lidney said. He checked. He clawed at the sweat with a hand.

'Yes,' Gently said.

'I can prove it,' Lidney said. 'I can bloody prove where I was.'

'But shall we believe it?' Gently said.

Lidney's mouth was a little open. His eyes weren't focusing on Gently. His eyes were frowning, pulled down at the outside corners. His featherlike cheeks looked waxy. He said:

'I can prove it all right. I know a way to prove that.'

'Depending on your knowledge of the time he was killed,' Gently said.

'I can prove it,' Lidney said 'I don't care what bloody time he was killed. I'm outside of it, every minute. I've got a witness you don't know about.'

'How convenient,' Gently said. 'Now you can tell us the whole story.'

'There isn't no story,' Lidney said.

'About the money for the dance hall,' Gently said. 'About the option falling in this week. About Harry French learning what you were up to. About his coming to your bungalow and getting killed with a hammer. About you blackmailing young French and Archer afterwards.'

'All that's squit I tell you,' Lidney said.

'Witnesses, young French and your cousins,' Gently said.

'I say it's squit, all squit,' Lidney said. 'There wasn't no blackmail, nothing like that. It was a business deal, that's all it was.'

'Oh yes,' Gently said, 'I don't suppose you threatened very much, just pointed out what a favour you were doing by keeping a still tongue. Then Archer invented a new job and bumped your wages and young French was ready to rob his father's estate to keep Sid's peculiar temper sweet.'

'It wasn't blackmail,' Lidney said.

'It wasn't business,' Gently said. 'It never was business from the start. I don't hear of any partnership deed.'

'We don't bother with that sort of crap round here,' Lidney said.

'So Harry French discovered,' Gently said. 'And that was the end of Harry French.'

Lidney breathed fast, didn't say anything.

'You went out of that bungalow,' Gently said. 'French got the better of you in the fight. Your wife took over. You went out. Later French went out, your wife hadn't fixed him. Later still you came back in. You'd nothing to say. You began drinking. When young French left the bungalow you were still drinking. And Harry French was floating in the river.'

'I don't know anything about that,' Lidney said.

'If you don't,' Gently said, 'who does?'

'You bugger,' Lidney said, 'you nice bugger.'

'Was it,' Gently said, 'your wife, who followed him out?'

Lidney's eyes were filmed, staring big. He shuffled a foot and moved his weight on it. The floodlight was throwing a big shadow behind him and because of his hump the shadow looked headless. He said:

'You, you keep Rhoda out of it.'

'Why should I?' Gently said. 'There's only young French to vouch for her.'

'You let Rhoda alone,' Lidney said.

'Is young French lying then?' Gently said.

'So he was there,' Lidney said.

'Of course he was there,' Gently said.

'I don't know what Rhoda did with him,' Lidney said. 'She switched him about, his old man didn't find him.'

'When he came looking for him,' Gently said.

'All right,' Lidney said, 'when he came looking for him.'

189

'When you had the fight in the passage,' Gently said.

Lidney felt for the chair. He sat.

'Go on,' Gently said, 'when you had the fight.'

'I threw the doorstopper at him,' Lidney said. 'The bastard knocked me down in my own house. I threw it at him. Hit his shoulder. In my own house that was. The big bastard. The big bastard. She come out and stopped us fighting. He wouldn't have lasted, the bloody slob. She came out, give him the key. She'd got the kid out of it. He never found him.'

'Yes,' Gently said.

'Like that,' Lidney said. 'The kid was round the place all the time. He knows she never followed the old man out. He was there. He was with her when I got back.'

'When you got back from where?' Gently said.

'She sent me out,' Lidney said. 'Reckoned she could handle him best on her own, get round him, smooth him down.'

'You went somewhere,' Gently said.

Lidney clawed at his sweat. 'Up the rond,' he said.

'Away from the bridge,' Gently said.

'Yes,' Lidney said, 'away from the bridge.'

'Did you meet anyone?' Gently said.

'As far as the mill,' Lidney said, 'I was fighting that bastard all the way. As far as the mill, that's where I went.'

'And you didn't meet anyone?' Gently said.

'Up at the mill,' Lidney said. 'I was standing there near the mill-dyke. I don't know how long I was standing there. There was a wireless on in Bob Tooke's cottage. The window was open, it was the news. Bob was sitting there mending a fishing pole. I didn't go up, say nothing to him.'

Gently looked at Joyce. Joyce got up, went out.

'Then you came back,' Gently said.

'The kid was with her when I got back,' Lidney said. 'It's right. I went in and got the bottle. I was still fighting him. They were yapping.'

'What did you see as you came back?' Gently said.

'What should I see?' Lidney said.

'You might have met someone,' Gently said, 'seen someone further down the path.'

'I didn't see anyone,' Lidney said.

'Perhaps a light?' Gently said.

Lidney screwed his eyes shut, passed his hand over them.

'What light did you see?' Gently said.

'You frigger,' Lidney said. 'You will have it, won't you?'

'Yes,' Gently said, 'I'll have it.'

'You bloody know I didn't do it,' Lidney said.

'I wouldn't be too certain,' Gently said.

Lidney kept his eyes screwed, said: 'The door was open. That's all I saw. Where they were working. The light shone out of it. I didn't see any more than that.'

'Quite sure?' Gently said.

'Much good may it do you,' Lidney said. 'They sent the right bastard on this job, you don't give an inch, do you?'

'So now what about a statement?' Gently said.

'You've got all the statement I'm giving you,' Lidney said.

'I'll dictate one for you,' Gently said. 'You can make your own corrections.'

Lidney looked at him, wiped the sweat.

Gently dictated the statement. Lidney listened. He didn't interrupt as Gently dictated. He sat leaning forward on the low chair with his long arms crossed on his short knees. Gently spoke slowly, distinctly. The pencil rustled over the paper. In Trafalgar Road outside it was becoming dark. So far Joyce hadn't returned. At the end of the statement Gently said to Lidney:

'Have you anything to add or alter?'

Lidney said, still leaning forward: 'Just type the shitting thing out, that's all.'

'If there are any substantial changes we'd like to have them now,' Gently said.

'If there were you'd know about them,' Lidney said. 'Never mind all the crap, let's get it over.'

The shorthand man went away to type the statement. Gently switched off the flood, lit his pipe. Parfitt had been smoking cigarettes, he smoked two more. Lidney didn't ask to smoke, didn't move. Parfitt looked at Gently once or twice without catching his eye. They could hear the typewriter pattering in another room. A moth flew in through the window, buzzed, tapped about the lamps. Parfitt watched the moth. Gently said very softly:

'When did you know who did it?'

Lidney moved his head, said: 'Just frig off.'

Gently blew smoke at the ceiling. 'Save me some trouble,' he said. 'You've given me plenty.'

'It's what you're paid for,' Lidney said.

192

'Who else knows,' Gently said, 'apart from Archer?'

Lidney sat still, didn't say anything, held his breathing in check. The moth went on butting at the light bulbs. Parfitt didn't watch it, frowned. The typing stopped. The shorthand man came back, handed the typed statement to Gently. Gently read it aloud to Lidney. Lidney got up impatiently, moved to the desk. The sweat had dried on his face, he wasn't puckering his eyes, he looked at the penstand, didn't look at Gently. Gently finished, said:

'Is that correct?'

'Give me the bastard here,' Lidney said.

Gently turned the statement towards him, Lidney took a pen from the penstand, dipped it, wrote splutteringly, made a blot, swore. He threw down the pen.

'Is that the bloody lot?' he said.

'Not quite,' Gently said. 'We haven't heard from our man yet.'

'Do you think I'd sling my hook, is that it?' Lidney said.

Gently didn't reply, took the statement, counter-signed it, relit his pipe. They waited. Joyce rang. Lidney had begun to sweat again. His eyes were sharp on the phone, he leaned his head forward towards it. Gently hung up, looked at Lidney, said:

'All right. You're clear for the moment.'

'So I should bloody think,' Lidney said.

'We'll run you home,' Gently said.

'Oh no,' Lidney said, 'you're not running me home.' His eyes needled at Gently. 'I've had enough of you buggers,' he said. 'I'm taking a bus. I'd walk home sooner. I'd sooner bloody crawl home.'

Parfitt said: 'You'll crawl into a cell Lidney if you give us any more of that sort of language.'

'You don't count,' Lidney said. 'You're just the boy. Pipe down. Listen to what he tells you.'

Parfitt got to his feet.

'Get out,' Gently said to Lidney.

The uniform man took Lidney's arm. Lidney kicked the chair aside, went out. When he was outside he reached round the uniform man and slammed the door. Parfitt rushed to the door.

'No,' Gently said.

'I'll smash his ugly face in,' Parfitt said.

'Then you'll do what he wants you to do,' Gently said. 'Come back and sit down, let him go.'

'But why are we letting him go?' Parfitt said. 'I'll slap a bloody charge on him if you won't.'

'It wouldn't do any good,' Gently said, 'come back and sit down. We've got what we want. Let him go.'

Parfitt turned, looked across at Gently.

'Order up some coffee,' Gently said.

'I don't want coffee,' Parfitt said. 'I want to hit someone.'

'But there's nobody to hit,' Gently said. 'Nobody.'

CHAPTER TEN

THUS GROWING LATE on the night of Saturday August 8th being a clear night with stars and the adumbrating glow of two cities being the night when yesterday's empty moorings were full and today's packed quays were empty when the same boats had gone to the same places though with different people but with the same ineptitudes; on such a night as was this Superintendent Gently took Harry French's launch took it unlighted out of the yacht basin into the river through the bridge. Because there were few boats not yet set forth because the people in them were fresh to it and so self-absorbed because Reuben had moved his fair to Wraxstead and because Gently used no lights Inspector Parfitt he only observed Gently's passage through the bridge watched the launch pull over to its left moor a faint shadow on the glimmer of water. Then Inspector Parfitt having looked long and hard lit a cigarette strolled off the bridge went to sit in the car as he had been instructed and took no more part in that matter at that time; while Superintendent Gently after mooring at the rond looping his orange painter where Harry French had looped the painter he crossed the rough ground turned left down the cinder path came to the gate of the Speltons' house went through it through the garden to the door of the house which was closed though lights showed in the office window; and knocked quietly twice on the door.

David Spelton answered the knock. He said nothing to Superintendent Gently but stood looking at him. Superintendent Gently after a few moments made to enter through the door and David Spelton fell back. Superintendent Gently went into the office and David Spelton followed him after closing the outer door. Behind the desk in the office Jack Spelton was sitting. He had a handmade cigarette in the corner of his mouth a tin of papers and cigarette roller in front of him also a box of matches and a full ashtray; he was squinting at the ashtray breaking spent matches into it didn't look at Gently when Gently entered didn't say anything to Gently drew at the cigarette broke matches. David Spelton threw himself on a chair. Gently sat on another chair. Apart from the snapping of the matches and David Spelton's breathing there was silence in the office for upwards of a minute. Then David Spelton jumped up, said:

'Are you just going to bloody sit there?'

Gently was watching Jack Spelton. Jack Spelton nostrilled smoke broke matches.

'You've been at John French,' David Spelton said. 'You've been at Sid Lidney all day. You've had him in Starmouth giving him hell, he's just back. Now you're here. So what's it about, why can't you tell us, why are you sitting there like a bloody post, why can't you say what you've got to say, do you think we're going to knock your block off?'

Gently looked at David Spelton, said: 'You're well abreast of our movements.'

'Christ and why not?' David Spelton said. 'What do you do round here that nobody notices? We know, everyone knows, you'll read it in the Press tomorrow morning, the pubs, the yards, the boats, the lot, why can't we know like everyone else.'

'Then you know as much as I can tell you,' Gently said.

'Then why don't you do something about it?' David Spelton said.

'I am doing something about it,' Gently said.

'Oh Christ then get on with it,' David Spelton said.

Jack Spelton opened the tobacco tin fed tobacco into the machine fed in a paper licked the paper rolled a cigarette.

'You've eliminated that lot haven't you,' David Spelton said. 'You thought it was Sid who did it for a long time. You've been trying to break him down, get a confession, but it didn't work, you couldn't hang it on him. And young French, it's the same with him, you tried hard but it wouldn't fit. That leaves us. It's got to be us. We're the only ones left. It's me or Jack. Why can't you make your mind up and get it over and pull out your bloody handcuffs and take us away?'

'Dave,' Jack Spelton said, 'Dave.'

'I don't care, that's what he's after,' David Spelton said. 'I knew from the first how it was going to be, right

197

from them pulling him out on our slipway. We were too bloody handy on the spot, they had to bring it home to us. We were right there, motive, opportunity, hammers, and he comes back into our slipway, points us out, it was us.'

'No Dave,' Jack Spelton said.

'Yes what could be neater?' David Spelton said. 'It's poetic justice, it's credible, rational, just get rid of the other suspects and there we are. Yes, that's justice, it'll look like justice, it's what they're paid for, they'll get congratulated. I'll congratulate them. Congratulations. You've done a wonderful job. Call the Black Maria.'

Jack Spelton lit the fresh cigarette broke the match in three dropped the pieces.

Gently said to Jack Spelton: 'Was your shed door open that night, around eleven or a few minutes after?'

'Of course it was bloody well open,' David Spelton said. 'How else did we get out to smash his skull?'

'Was it open?' Gently said.

Jack Spelton looked into the ashtray. He nodded.

'Now you've made him happy,' David Spelton said. 'That was the last link. Case complete.'

'Why was it open?' Gently said.

Jack Spelton shook his head over the ashtray.

'Oh tell him tell him,' David Spelton said.

'It was open,' Jack Spelton said.

'So now you know the truth,' David Spelton said. 'Jackie never told a lie in his life, did he?'

'Dave,' Jack Spelton said.

'And it was me who went through that door,' David Spelton said.

Gently said nothing. Jack Spelton broke matches. David Spelton stood fronting Gently, swayed on his toes. David Spelton's brown hands were clenching and unclenching and his lips were quivering his nostrils expanded. Gently took no notice of David Spelton. Jack Spelton took no notice of his brother. A fretwork clock ticked on the wall. Jack Spelton squinted at the clock, said:

'You come here for someone.'

'Yes,' Gently said.

'Maybe they don't want to go,' Jack Spelton said.

'I could call in help,' Gently said.

'Maybe you could,' Jack Spelton said.

'Maybe you'd better,' David Spelton said. 'You won't take me in like a bloody lamb. I reckon you slipped up coming here on your lonesome, there's plenty of hammers in this establishment.'

'I'm only interested in one hammer,' Gently said, 'and that's probably in the river just out there.'

'Maybe we could arrange for you to look for it,' David Spelton said. 'I could arrange it, I know how it's done.'

'Dave, Dave,' Jack Spelton said.

'Yes,' David Spelton said, 'it's a quiet night. It was quiet on Tuesday when the fair shut down. It's quieter tonight. Nobody about, very quiet.'

'You go and sit down Dave,' Jack Spelton said.

'I'd better go and be looking for a hammer,' David Spelton said.

Gently said: 'Yes you do that. Go and look for a hammer.'

'What?' David Spelton said, 'what? What?'

Gently glanced at him. David Spelton's eyes were staring. He went back on his heels, flat-footed. His mouth was dragged, had a wisp of foam on the lips.

'Dave,' Jack Spelton said, 'the bloke's only doing his job.'

'I'll,' David Spelton said, 'I'll . . .'

'He isn't being kidded,' Jack Spelton said.

'He's alone here,' David Spelton said. 'Just like Harry French was alone. He doesn't have some bloody magic on account of he's a ferret. He's an enemy, like Harry French was. He's my enemy. He wants to lock me up. Why have I got to sit around waiting for it, why have I, why have I?'

'It isn't good enough Dave,' Jack Spelton said.

'It's got to be good enough,' David Spelton said.

Jack Spelton lisped smoke. 'It had to pan out this way,' he said. 'You knew it, I knew it, you're only spitting blood Dave.'

David Spelton looked at his brother. Jack Spelton broke a match. His thin face was long, the cheeks indrawn, hollow. He squinted suddenly at David Spelton, didn't hold his eye. David Spelton groaned. He fell into a chair, went slack.

Gently said to Jack Spelton: 'Is there anything you want to tell me?'

Jack Spelton shook his head. 'Reckon it's your job,' he said.

'You could make it easier,' Gently said.

'Don't want to make it easier,' Jack Spelton said. 'You just work it out old partner, I'm not going to draw lines for you.'

'Let's say you'd make it easier for everyone,' Gently said.

Jack Spelton shook his head, said nothing.

'If that's how you want it then,' Gently said. He rose slowly, stood looking at Jack Spelton. 'I'm going down to Lidney's for a few minutes,' he said.

Jack Spelton squinted towards him, towards his chest. He poked ends of matches into the filled ashtray, looked at his brother. His brother was still.

'There's something Lidney can tell me,' Gently said, 'I don't think we'll need anything else. Then I'll be back. I've a car waiting at the bridge. Perhaps you'll help me just a little bit. That'd be best.'

Jack Spelton said nothing, went on poking. The fretwork clock fizzed, chimed tinnily. The hands of the clock pointed to eleven hours. Gently turned to the door, went out of the office.

He walked firmly, didn't look about him, listened to his steps crunching on the cinders. There were stars but there was no moon and there were no lights except back at the bridge. Across the rough rond where the launch was moored the river lay dark as a river of ink and very low and very indistinct on the surface curled and twisted the phantom mist. He heard no sound but his footsteps. He came to the seventh bungalow, pushed open the gate. A room was lit in the front of the bungalow and light spilled on the mooring cut but the cut was empty. Gently rapped at the door. He heard a man's voice inside. Steps came towards the door, the door was opened. Lidney stood inside the door. His eyes peered

201

out. He stood heavy and large with the light behind him. Gently said:

'I'll step in for a moment.'

'You,' Lidney said hoarsely, 'you again.'

'I shan't be here for long,' Gently said. 'Not as long as Harry French was here on Tuesday.'

Lidney stepped back. The light fell on his face. His face was yellowish, he was snatching at his breath. Behind him down the hallway stood Rhoda Lidney her hair in curlers her mouth sagged open. Gently went in, closed the door after him. He went down the hallway past Rhoda Lidney. Rhoda Lidney's eyes stared at him, she said nothing. He went into the parlour, stood, took out his pipe. Lidney came in. Lidney stood not looking at Gently. Rhoda Lidney came in. Gently lit his pipe. Lidney said:

'You're going to pinch me after all.'

'No, nothing of that sort,' Gently said.

'Not a pinch?' Lidney said.

'Just ten minutes to smoke my pipe,' Gently said.

'Smoke your pipe,' Lidney said. 'Why do you have to smoke your pipe here?'

'That's all I'm going to do,' Gently said, 'you don't have to stand around and watch me.'

'It's some bloody game,' Lidney said.

'I told you you were in the clear,' Gently said.

'Yes, it bloody looks like it, doesn't it?' Lidney said.

'Are you going to turn me out?' Gently said.

He smoked. Rhoda Lidney came further into the room. She looked at Gently, looked at her husband. Lidney was twisting his mouth, his long arms hanging.

His eyes were unpuckered, looking at nothing. Rhoda Lidney said:

'That frigging pipe stinks.'

'Don't you come anything,' Lidney muttered.

'I'll say what I like,' Rhoda Lidney said. 'He can't come buggering us about like this.'

'You button your lip,' Lidney said. 'This bastard never does nothing without there's a reason. Let him smoke his pipe, button your lip.'

'Well I'm not scared of him,' Rhoda Lidney said.

She went to a chair, dumped herself on it. Gently looked at his watch, smoked. Rhoda Lidney began twisting more curlers into her hair, her eyes fixed all the time on Gently. Lidney didn't move from where he stood. There weren't any sounds from outside the room. Rhoda Lidney finished putting in curlers. Gently looked at his watch again, slipped his pipe in his pocket. He said:

'Thanks. I'll be going.'

'How nice to have seen you,' Rhoda Lidney said.

Lidney twisted his head, stared up at Gently. He shook his head, said nothing.

Gently went down the hallway, out of the door, closed the door and gate behind him. Outside the gate he paused, listened, waited for his vision to readjust. Then he walked slowly along the cinder path and across the rough ground to the launch. He stood by the launch. He stood facing the river. He stood with his back towards the path. He listened. He heard a faint breeze lifting the leaves of a bush willow. He heard a car come up to the bridge, halt, accelerate over the bridge. He heard a coot-call from up the river and the splash of a rising fish from down the river and the very distant rumble of a train and the whistling flight of a swan overhead. Then for some time he heard only the bush willow and when the breeze failed, silence. He moved. He bent down to untie the painter. He had his hands at the painter. He heard close behind him a tremulous whimper like the whimper of a dog. He turned quickly, turned aside, snatched a torch from his pocket, shone the torch. The torch beam fell on Vera Spelton. Vera Spelton had a hammer raised in her hand. Vera Spelton was frowning flinching dribbling whimpering buzzing through her teeth making feints with the hammer. She came for the light. She struck at the light. Gently wasn't behind the light. He grabbed her wrist. She whimpered, twisted free, suddenly threw herself away from him, seemed to vanish. He swung the beam of the torch about, it didn't find her. It fell on the upturned boat. From beneath the boat came a whimper.

Gently advanced to the boat, played his torch on it. Inside the boat Vera Spelton buzzed and whined. The rond where the boat lay was uneven and below the gunnel at one point was a shallow gap. The gap was no larger than the entrance to a fox earth and it was scuffed and worn bare of grass and when Gently shone the torch on it the whinings increased and retreated further under the boat. He played the torch about the rond, found a length of old plank. He inserted the end of the plank in the gap, got his shoulder under the plank, heaved. The boat lifted. Vera Spelton whimpered. He heaved again, threw his weight against the boat. The boat tottered, came to the point of balance, poised, went over crashingly in the nettles. Vera Spelton set up a high-pitched keening. She was crouched to the ground still clutching the hammer. There were other tools about her. There were pieces of mahogany boat fitments bolts screws a model of a yacht. On a stick thrust in the ground was tied a Spelton houseflag. On an offcut of pegboard were pinned photographs of yachts. Vera Spelton keened at Gently. She held the hammer out in front of her. Her lips were pulled back over her teeth spittle dripped from her chin she hitched herself along the ground away from him held the hammer between them. Gently said:

'You're up late Miss Spelton.'

Vera Spelton whimpered, feinted with the hammer.

'You should have been in bed long ago,' Gently said. 'Your brothers will be worried about you. Dave and Jackie will be worried.'

Vera Spelton whined at him. She bubbled spittle.

'You're losing your beauty sleep,' Gently said. 'Attractive girls like you should go to bed early, they shouldn't stay out in the night air. You mustn't do it very often Miss Spelton. You want to stay attractive don't you? This is really very late, you should think about bed, then you'll be attractive for tomorrow.'

Vera Spelton stared at the light, didn't make a noise. Gently let the beam fall between them. He kept an eye on the hammer. The hammer was still. The head of the hammer had sunk a little. Gently said:

'You're a good girl, Miss Spelton. You wanted to save your brothers a lot of trouble. You came out specially just now to save them from trouble. You didn't mind staying up late to do that for them. You're a good girl, you've done well. Now Dave and Jackie don't have to worry any longer. You've taken care of them, you're a true Spelton. You've made everything all right by coming out here like this.'

The head of the hammer sank further.

'I'm going to tell them about you,' Gently said, 'how brave you've been, how you got rid of their enemies, we'll go in now and I'll tell them. Give me the hammer and we'll go in. They won't be angry any longer. I'll show them the hammer, tell them all about it. Look, here's my hand. Give me the hammer.'

He held out his hand, shone the torch on it. Vera Spelton was silent.

'Put the hammer in my hand,' Gently said.

Vera Spelton reached out, put the hammer in his hand.

The hammer was a three-pound ball-peen hammer and there were bloodstains on the head of the hammer and on the edge of the face of the hammer was a burr and in the burr was trapped a pluck of hair. The haft was burned with the Spelton brand. Gently handled the hammer by the helm of the haft. He held the hammer behind him away from Vera Spelton. He made a sweeping motion with the torch.

'Come on then,' he said.

Vera Spelton rose silently. The light touched her face. She was smiling. She didn't say anything. Gently didn't touch her. He began to walk. She walked beside him. They walked across the rough ground and down the cinder path and through the garden of the Spelton house. Gently opened the door without knocking. They passed through into the office.

'Here's your sister,' Gently said.

Vera Spelton smiled at her brothers. Gently laid the hammer on the desk. Vera Spelton sat. She kept smiling.

Nobody spoke for a little while. Jack Spelton had stopped smoking. David Spelton sat folded up, his face turned aside. Neither of them looked at Vera Spelton. Vera Spelton didn't look at them. She was smiling at something a long way off. Her hands were folded in her lap and the hands were still and she sat still. At last Jack Spelton said thickly:

'She's one of our hammers I reckon.'

'Don't touch the hammer,' Gently said.

'Wasn't going to touch it,' Jack Spelton said. 'I was wondering where she'd got to.'

'You didn't tell us one was missing,' Gently said.

'No, I didn't,' Jack Spelton said. 'That's one of the old hammers, that is. Somebody hasn't been using it fair.'

He closed his eyes.

'She likes tools,' he said.

David Spelton straightened, stared at the hammer.

'She can use them too,' Jack Spelton said. 'I taught her that, how to use tools. You see these things. She made them all. All the angles cut clean. She's a clinker at using tools. I could take her on tomorrow.'

'Oh shut up,' David Spelton said.

'Using tools,' Jack Spelton said. 'She's got the feel for it. It's in her. She loves wood, a bit of wood.'

207

'Jack shut up shut up,' David Spelton said.

'She loves the yachts,' Jack Spelton said. 'You won't tear her away from them, not the yachts, they're everything to her. She can't live without them.'

'I'll go mad, shut up,' David Spelton said.

'You see her sail one,' Jack Spelton said.

David Spelton gave a cry, covered his eyes with his hands.

'Dave taught her sailing,' Jack Spelton said. 'Dave's the master one for that.'

He didn't say anything else just then. He hadn't opened his eyes this while. He sat as though staring at the hammer on the desk but without his eyes open, not moving.

'How many knew?' Gently said. 'This isn't evidence, doesn't matter.'

David Spelton said through his teeth: 'All of them knew, everybody.'

'Lidney knew,' Gently said.

'Sid knew,' David Spelton said.

'Archer,' Gently said.

'He'd know,' David Spelton said.

'Suppose I'd charged one of them,' Gently said.

David Spelton shook his head.

'Tell me this,' Gently said, 'was she ever violent before?'

David Spelton moaned, rocked his shoulders. He lifted his head, looked at Gently.

'Was she?' Gently said.

David Spelton said: 'Blame me.'

'There's no point in blaming anyone,' Gently said.

'Yes,' David Spelton said, 'because I'm to blame. She never hated anyone. She doesn't know how to. I'm to blame. It's my hate killed him. She heard me talk. She caught it off me. It was my hate saw him there, took that hammer, I struck the blow, I killed him. She's gentle, wouldn't hurt a fly. Don't take her. Take me.'

'You know that's impossible,' Gently said.

'But it isn't impossible,' David Spelton said. 'You thought I did it, you might have charged me too, you want justice, that is justice, I'm responsible, I'll go with you.'

'No,' Gently said.

'But why, why?' David Spelton said. 'Look at her. She's not the violent one. I'm the violent one. I always have been.'

'She can be violent,' Gently said.

'Only because of me,' David Spelton said. 'If I'm not here she'll be all right, it's me who's the trouble, me who's to blame.'

'You're to blame for anger, hatred,' Gently said, 'not for what's been done, you're not responsible for that. She's not responsible either, we shan't hold her responsible. But she's a danger to others. We can't pass it by.'

'Through me she's a danger,' David Spelton said. 'She's all right on her own, look, she's all right.'

'No,' Gently said, 'I've seen her otherwise, perhaps you have too. She'll have to go with me.'

Jack Spelton said: 'She can't be happy. Not away from us.'

'She'll be afraid,' David Spelton said. 'She must have us. She must.'

'This is her life,' Jack Spelton said, 'all she knows, all

she is, the three of us here, that's V, she'll die like a bird if she's put in a cage. She's happy here, always happy. She's like one of them birds what chip in the reeds. Don't take her away, give her to strangers. She wouldn't last. Leave her here.'

'It doesn't rest with me,' Gently said.

'We'll take care of her, watch her,' Jack Spelton said. 'Hull that hammer in the river, I'd have hulled it in if I'd found it. You can make up some yarn about what happened. You don't want to take her away.'

'I'm sorry,' Gently said, 'I mean I'm sorry.'

'That'd be the crime,' Jack Spelton said.

'She'll maybe come back again,' Gently said, 'you'll maybe get custody, it'll all be considered.'

'She wants the sun, the water,' Jack Spelton said, 'the boats. Where's she going to get them?'

'They won't be unkind to her,' Gently said.

'Where's she going to get us?' Jack Spelton said.

Gently didn't say anything. He looked at Vera Spelton. Vera Spelton had heard nothing. Where she was smiling was across the Sounds across the sandhills perhaps across the sea. She was very beautiful very young very like David Spelton. David Spelton was weeping. Vera Spelton smiled.

'Do I,' Jack Spelton said, 'do I pack her some things?'

'Some night things,' Gently said. 'They'll let you know what to send later.'

'I'll go and do it,' Jack Spelton said, 'I'll go and pack V's things.'

He got up, knocked against the desk, steadied himself, went out.

* * *

When they arrived at the car they found Parfitt asleep. Jack Spelton was carrying a big fibre suitcase, a woollen cardigan, a raincoat. Vera Spelton was walking beside Gently. David Spelton came behind them. Vera Spelton had remained silent though both of her brothers had spoken to her. Gently carried the hammer wrapped in a newspaper. The time was between twelve and one o'clock. They met nobody. There was no traffic. There were no lights. The night was still. Parfitt woke, said:

'Sorry sir. Must have got into a doze.'

Gently grunted, opened a door, stood aside, glanced at Vera Spelton. Vera Spelton slipped quietly into the car. When she'd got in it she sat rigidly. Parfitt saw the suitcase, jumped out smartly, unlocked the boot, stowed the suitcase. Nothing was said. The Speltons stood woodenly. Jack Spelton glanced towards the bridge. Gently laid the hammer on the seat, got in behind with Vera Spelton. Parfitt returned to the driver's seat, slammed the door. The night air had an edge of chilliness. The stars were sharp, over-numerous. Gently closed his door, lowered the window.

Jack Spelton said: 'We'll, we'll hear.'

'You'll be kept informed,' Gently said. 'You'll be able to see her when you like.'

'Yes. Yes, I reckon so,' Jack Spelton said.

Parfitt started the engine.

'Anything else?' Gently said.

'No,' Jack Spelton said, 'nothing else.'

'We'll get away,' Gently said.

He closed the window. Parfitt let in the clutch. The car drove off. That was it.

★ ★ ★

And it was still fine weather on Sunday August 9th because of an anticyclone which remained stationary and would continue to remain stationary over the North Sea: a rare occurrence once in ten summers at or about August Bank Holiday happening this year this summer during these days this dying. Raising the night mists the early dew framing the white morning sun heating the ocean the reeded rivers the broads meres pulks deeks yachts wet-awninged tall-masted alder willow sweet briar banks mint-odoured flower-bosked and the white waterlily: all birds such as reed warblers reed pheasants the coughing bittern the musical swan the harsh harnser the flirting waterhen the sad coot: yellow black-trellised soaring swallowtails fragrant-winged drooping dragon-flies damselflies skidding boatmen the bold water-walking arachnid: setting staring wide the day of these and many other things also leaving the twilight beautiful and the night prickling with stars: though he was this was now not so was other, though was still this.

Thus: Superintendent Gently returned to London having given the local police his expert advice and the case was referred considered adjourned reopened recon-sidered appealed disposed. Of which matters Superin-tendent Gently heard nothing nor indeed attempted to hear anything though some of the details of the case would come to mind when it was fine summer weather.

Thus and thus.

Being an end.